The Crying Bird

A Novel

E.J.Stillings

Published by Emily Jordan Stillings

ISBN-13: 978-0-9985256-0-0

Special thanks to God for absolutely everything.

This book is dedicated to Mary DelleFave.
Thank you for loving and supporting me through
all my creative adventures.

This book is also dedicated to anyone
who has ever experienced grief.

Table of Contents

CHAPTER ONE

The End?

I look at the check for one and a half million dollars made payable to me, May Johnson. This is my compensation for the wrongful death of my daughter. I put it back in the drawer of the foyer table.

The kettle screams almost in harmony with the whistling wind of the snowstorm outside. I move it to a different burner and turn off the stove. I'm not in the mood for tea anymore.

It's been too long since I've seen her, my beautiful Annie, and not long enough since she passed. I don't know how I'm supposed to feel. Part of me is broken, and the other wants to go somewhere busy, with people going about their lives, hoping to distract myself, but I always stay home. Can I still call it a home now I'm alone?

My husband, Dave, died five years ago from a heart attack. That morning was like any other. He kissed my forehead while I was busy cleaning up after breakfast and said, "Until I see you again." It's almost funny now, and I think it still holds true, but how I wish I would have looked into his eyes and told him I love him dearly.

We were teenage sweethearts, married at eighteen and after twelve —yes, twelve— years of trying, we finally conceived our daughter. At least he got ten years with our daughter before he died. Not that it matters any more, I guess.

When Annie turned fifteen, she begged me to let her go to summer camp. I admit I held her too close. She needed to explore and get into trouble and just be a teenager, but I was scared of being alone even then. She would ask me, 'What could go wrong?' as if she didn't know me at all, though she would tell you herself we were best friends. And we were. So, even though I knew of a million things that could go wrong, it was the yearning look in her eyes that made me say yes. She had her father's eyes.

There were no cell phones allowed at camp. I swear I bit all of my fingernails off when she told me that part, but I tried to be cool because she thought it was cool. Like the 'old days', each kid was required to write one letter home each week, but my sweet girl wrote one the first day so I would get it sooner:

Hey May-May! Camp is everything I hoped!! I mean, it's just like in the movies! The only thing missing is you!!! We are sleeping in a cabin full of bunk beds and we ate in a 'mess hall' which totally lives up to its name! This

1

one kid, David, started a food fight and I got mashed potatoes up my nose! Gross right? It was so much fun though. I made a friend already too! Her name is Carly and she looks like a barbie-doll but she can name every kind of bug, which I thought was weird at first but then I realized it's just her thing and I like her more for it.

I hope you are having fun too and if you're not, then you need to call Aunt Brenda! You know she loves to hang out with you, so.... HANG OUT WITH BRENDA!

Don't miss me too much. I miss you enough for the both of us, but I'm also having so much fun. Do the same, ok? I love you with all my heart and soul! Tomorrow I'll be zipping down a zip line in the woods! Wish me luck!

Love, Love, Love,
Annie

I try to picture how she might have looked in her last moments on the zip line before her life ended: brown eyes twinkling, the warm sun shining on her face, wisps of golden brown hair caressing her cheeks in the wind. Her lips, coated in cherry flavored gloss, stretching wide into the most radiant smile of her life.

Damn it, I miss her so much. I wish she didn't go on that stupid zip line! Stupid, stupid zip line. Stupid camp. One person doesn't do their job right and while my baby girl is sailing through the woods, a cord gets wrapped around her neck and snaps it. At least it was instant, I guess. That's what people tell me anyway, but why her? Why Annie, when a dozen other kids supposedly zipped before her? ...I can't think about it...

I curl into a fetal position in bed and fall asleep still holding the letter.

∞ ● ∞

A woman's voice fills my bedroom, "C'mon, old lady. Up and at'em!"

Just freaking great. It's Brenda, my once lovable but now utterly annoying younger sister. She flings open the curtains then hurls herself across the room and onto me on the bed.

I yell, "Go away!"

She nudges me, "Rise and shine, birthday girl."

It's my birthday? Ugh, why does she have to remind me?

She gets me showered and dressed the way she does every time she visits now. I don't mind it that much, though she always complains about the smell, but I don't smell anything.

Sipping my coffee, I stare at the kitchen window as my sister yammers on. I used to like looking out the window, but the panes of glass are so dirty now I can't. It's fine, the random patterns of grime more suitable for thinking about *not* thinking about things.

"May? Maisie?" Brenda snaps her fingers.

Only Dave ever called me Maisie. My name is actually May. Brenda would joke that our parents had a lapse of creativity when it came to me so they named me after the month I was born. It's not even true. Well I was born in May, but they were wildly creative. My middle name is Flower. Yep, May Flower, because that's when the flowers bloom around here. I see how they came up with it.

I don't like it when she uses his nickname for me, but then again, she calls me every name she thinks of, especially when trying to get my attention. I continue to ignore her.

Annie called me May-May, which was my favorite because she used to say, 'everyone says mom or mommy or mama, but only I have a May-May'. Brenda's lucky she didn't try that one today. I would have thrown my coffee mug at her. I picture my mug knocking her in the head and smile.

"You know," She turns to me, spatula in hand, "ever since Dave died you lost your spunk."

My smile drops and I glare at her.

She continues cooking. "I know, I know… you think you didn't because you goofed off with Annie, but I know you. And, now that she's….Well, it's been long enough. Neither one of them would want you living like this. It's not living at all." She sets a plate of eggs and burnt toast on the table in front of me.

This is the best thing she's cooked yet, truly, but now I'm definitely not hungry.

She has that look on her face, probing me with her eyes, showing me she cares. I know she cares. She's been coming over too often, for I don't know how long, to bring me groceries and make sure my bills are paid. I'm sick of it. It would be easier to appreciate her help if she weren't so damn annoying.

I stir the watery 'sunny-side-up' eggs with my fork and notice, through a small clean spot on the window, the snow really has stopped falling and the sun is shining. Maybe I'll go outside today, if Brenda ever leaves.

She appears in front of me, smiling and wide eyed, holding the settlement check in front of my face, "When did this come?"

I shrug.

"We should go shopping! It'll get you out of the house and take your mind off—"

I throw my fork at her and stomp out of the kitchen, up the stairs, into my bedroom and slam the door. I pace around my room, fists clenched, and breathing like I'm practicing for birth. How dare she? She's got no sense of boundaries! I don't care if it's my birthday or she's my only living relative. She crossed the line. 'Go shopping' she says. Unbelievable.

Was that the front door? I look out my bedroom window and down at the driveway. Brenda's getting in her car. Good riddance. When her car is halfway down the street, I go downstairs and out onto the porch.

This is the first time I've been outside in a long time, I guess. The sun looks refreshing. I step out onto the driveway, point my face to the sky and close my eyes. Dave and Annie loved the outdoors, and all things nature.

We went camping one time for some fresh air and a change of scenery, a trip I was kind of forced into. It's not that I dislike nature, I just think nature doesn't like me very much. While they enjoyed themselves, I got bit and stung by every kind of bug, stepped in every kind of animal poop and got attacked by a squirrel, a lizard and a bird. In one trip. The message was clear to me, so now I keep my distance.

I open my eyes. A flock of birds are flying overhead. I've never cared for birds and their expressionless faces, and their ability to fly while I'm stuck on the ground.

A wet blob plops onto my forehead and I know exactly what it is. I flip the birds a bird of my own.

For the first time since I can remember, I look at myself in the bathroom mirror. Who is this graying, wrinkling woman with bird poop on her forehead?

∞ • ∞

I'm trying to settle back into my grieving routine, but every day I have this feeling I can't put into words. I think I'm hungry, so I eat, but I still feel it. I think I"m tired, so I sleep, sometimes all day and night, but when I wake up I still feel it.

"Damn it, Brenda," I say to the ceiling fan in the living room that wobbles and clicks with each rotation. I can almost see her annoying face in the middle of it… Why is it even on?

I go stare at the framed family pictures hanging on the wall, now cockeyed and dusty. We were so happy. I mean, sure, we had rough times, but we were a unit, bonded by blood. Emptiness starts to take over again and it feels good in a way, familiar now.

My sister pops back into my thoughts. I grunt as I sit down on the floor and start pulling photo albums from the book cases back in the living room, strewing them all around me. I'm looking for something, but I don't know what it is.

The doorbell rings. There's a man's silhouette through the sheer curtain over the glass door. I stay sitting on the floor, surrounded by memories. He knocks on the door, "Mrs. Johnson? It's your neighbor, Carmichael."

No one has come to the door since the wave of concerned casseroles right after the neighborhood heard the news about Annie. Besides that, no one apparently cared. What could he possibly want? Ugh. Maybe he'll just go away.

He's pressed against the glass. "I can see you."

Shit. I drag myself up off the floor then open the door a crack.

He jumps. "Are uh…are you ok?"

I clear my throat and raise my chin, "I'm very busy, what do you want?"

While he stammers for the right words, I see my grass behind him, that's grown bushy and is blanketed in fall leaves.

He continues, "I was just wondering if you're going to tend to your yard before it snows again? I don't want to have the same problems we had last year."

I glare at him. I've gotten quite good at glaring. Why hasn't Brenda done anything with the lawn? She's sticking her nose into everything else.

"I understand now what you're going though… My dog died recently,"

"You poor thing," I say with a complete lack of sincerity. I don't know how I even mustered those words, what I wanted to say was, are you freaking kidding me right now?

"But we are still living and we still need to care for our homes…" He looks at my hair, "and ourselves, ya'know?"

Not another one. I'm being bombarded with idiots who don't know a damn thing about what I'm going through. I slam the door and lock it. Then I no sooner get back on the floor when I hear the door unlock and in comes freaking Brenda.

I snap, "What is with you people?"

"Nice to see you too."

"You should try knocking for once! You're always barging into *my* house, *my* life!"

"I'm trying to be a good sister and help you in your time of need—which has gone on too long, in my opinion. Yes, it's hard losing the ones we love, and we will always have that hurt in our hearts, but life really does go on."

"You're a nuisance!" I hate it when she does that, like it's her loss too. She didn't give birth to my Annie.

"Fine, that settles it. I'm not coming over any more, if you haven't noticed already these past months. I love you, you know I do, but it's time for you to take care of yourself again."

"Good."

She sighs. "All right, well, before I go, I want to make sure you know I deposited your settlement check into your account for you. I set up your bills to pay automatically from your bank account. Now you're a millionaire I thought that would be easiest. Have you even checked your mail since the last time I came over?"

I fold my arms and purse my lips.

"See? I worry about you. What would you do without me checking on you?"

I'm glaring at her so hard my face hurts.

"Fine. Don't forget to eat and, you know, shower. I'm not coming back until you call me, and there better be a please and thank you involved." She locks the door behind her.

Her footsteps fade. I lay flat on my back and stare at the stupid Brenda ceiling fan. There's a difference between support and treating someone like a child. I'm hurting and she freaking makes it worse. Couldn't she come and take care of things without talking to me? Whatever. I can take care of myself. I take a deep breath and close my eyes.

Footsteps clunk up to the door. My eyes shoot open. I listen. The door unlocks.

"One more thing—"

"Damn it, Brenda!" I shoot to my feet too fast and get dizzy, but I don't let that stop me. Stumbling to keep myself standing I continue to point at her and yell, "You've got no sense! You're a lousy sister, abandoning me now!" I step on the corner of my thickest photo album, my ankle rolls and I tumble over, face first into the side of the glass coffee table. The last thing I remember is hearing the glass shattering.

CHAPTER TWO

White Butterflies

I wake up in a bed under an unfamiliar ceiling with fluorescent lights. My vision is blurry, but I know I'm surrounded by nurses who are nodding and scribbling notes. Great, a teaching hospital, just what I need.

Though I can't make out what the doctor is saying yet, I'm sure it goes something like, 'Looky here folks at this miserable woman. Take pity on her. *Learn* from her'.

They notice I'm awake and crowd in closer. The doctor is the closest, so his face comes into focus. He's younger than I am with tan lines on his face from sunglasses, probably his first day back from a vacation in Florida, playing golf and fishing. I kind of hate him. I'm pretty sure he means well, but he's got that same probing look on his face Brenda gets when she's intent on knowing how I'm doing.

"Mrs. Johnson, can you hear me?"

I nod.

"You took quite a fall yesterday, but you don't have any serious injuries, not even a concussion, though you did pass out. The wounds on your face should heal nicely with minimal scarring. Other than that, we monitored you throughout the night and you're doing fine. You're free to go when ready."

What the hell does he know about how I'm doing? It's customary to ask a person how they're doing, not assume. People don't get it. The sun down in Florida must have fried his brain.

The parade of white coats leaves the room. My vision is almost back, but my right eye won't open all the way. Oh well, it doesn't matter.

Brenda comes into view on my left. It must be obvious my right eye is messed up. She shoves a mirror in front of my face and whispers sternly like our mother used to do, "This is what you've done to yourself!" She starts to cry and drops the mirror on my bed.

I didn't see myself when she was holding it, because she was more or less jerking it around in front of my face the way a person would shove a half-eaten shoe in the face of a dog, as if to say, 'Look what you've done! Bad, May! Bad, bad, May!"

I'm curious to see now, not that I really care. I pick up the mirror. What in the— I look like Frankenstein's freaking bride! My face is covered in white butterfly bandages, I have a knot on my forehead, my right eye is puffy and I'm all pale and bruised.

A thought pops into my head: maybe I'll start a new trend and when something bad happens they'll say they've had a 'May-Day'. I crack a smile. She notices.

"You think this is funny? God, help you, May..."

I get out of bed, my bare bottom showing through the back of the hospital gown, grab my pajamas and lock myself in the bathroom. I try to send a mental note to her to go away, but when I emerge, she's still here, standing in front of the door.

She says, "I think you should see someone. We are all we've got left in the world and I'm worried about you."

I hadn't realized freaking *Brenda* is truly all I've got left now. I kind of feel bad for her too if I'm all she's got left. Wait, I thought she was getting married? Eh, things must not have worked out between them and she's never said anything because of everything I'm going through... Who am I kidding? I'm probably the reason she's alone now too. I can't believe she let me ruin her life. She's an idiot.

"Don't dump your baggage on me, like I don't have enough!" I push past her. "Go away. Go live your life!"

Stomping down the hall in my old pajamas, with my 'rat's nest' hair and bandaged face, I'm muttering to myself and flailing my arms, then I accidentally say out loud, "Damn it, Brenda, you really know how to push my buttons!"

There's a desk with a few young nurses working at computers. Talking to none of them in particular, I ask, "How do I get out of here? Brenda keeps bothering me." I point back toward the room I came from. She's not there like I expected.

The people at the desk are staring at me like I'm a

TV playing some dramatic scene, so I keep walking down the hall and go through a pair of double doors. I'm so irritated I can't even focus on getting out of here.

I get in an elevator and lean in the corner with my head bowed. I'm the only one in here so I take the opportunity to close my eyes and yell loud enough for the universe to hear my plea, "Leave me alone, Brenda!"

The doors open. There's a security officer. She's a woman about my age and hesitates getting in here with me. She takes one step in and looks around, then pushes a button and stands next to me.

I ask her, "Can you help me get out of here? Before Brenda finds me? I can't find my way out."

She doesn't make eye contact, but talks into her walkie talkie, "Yeah, I got her."

Oh good, those kids at the desk must have called me an escort. My head is throbbing now so I cradle it in my hands and try to focus on my breathing.

The doors open and the guard ushers me to walk with her, "Come on. Let's go."

Walking with her, I keep my eyes on the ground as we make our way down the hall, around the corner, through a couple of doors, then stop.

"Wait here," She says.

The room is full of people that are a little on the loony side of sanity. I blink a couple times, but everything's still the same. The guard is almost out the door, so I stand up and yell, "Hey, you can't leave me here," but she doesn't even turn around. Maybe this is where I belong now.

I slump into a chair next to an older gentleman, if you can call him that with drool running down his chin. He's playing a game of checkers by himself, but his moves don't even make sense. He'll pick up a random black chip and move it to a different spot, then pick up a red chip and put it in his mouth. Annie would have liked his creativity. At least he's quiet company.

It's pretty easy to figure out the cliques in here: the rowdy bunch are in the far corner, then at the window are the ones who are talking and talking, and the quiet ones are here by me with the board games. I mean, they still make some noises, but their mouths are full of game pieces, so, it's ok. Maybe I could stay here. Then I could get the nurses to make Brenda leave.

Something about the place felt comfortable enough to fall asleep. I'll never do that again... I woke not five minutes later with a slimy checker piece on the knot on my forehead and the old man about to plop another one into my gaping mouth. All the quiet board game players start laughing hysterically. I throw the checker chip across the room and it rolls under a nurse's feet.

Oh, a nurse! She shuts herself into the room by the door. There's a counter, so I straighten myself up and go over. "Can you page Brenda?"

She looks at me, then a piece of paper in front of her, "Brenda, huh?"

"Yes. Brenda." I'm getting annoyed now that I don't want to be here anymore.

"Sure..." she says, long and high-pitched.

I don't like the way she said it, like consoling a crazy—oh, no. "I'm not crazy. I mean, I've had my moments, but I'm only in here because I bumped my head."

"Mhm."

"Doctor what's-his-name... um... he's young with tan lines from his sunglasses, he said I could leave when

14

ready. Oh, and by the way, Brenda is my sister. I'm May Flower—I mean, May Johnson—Johnson's my married name, but my husband died. I kept the name. Flower is my middle name." Great, I'm rambling, I'll be out of here in no time.

I'm given a little blue pill, which I could have tried harder to refuse, but I haven't had a valium in a long time. Now I'm practically drooling with the rest of the loonies.

I visit the window clique and chat for a few minutes. We all agree aliens exist. Then I lackadaisically jump in place for a while with the rowdy group. One of them keeps screaming, "Fly, birdie, fly! Fly, birdie, fly!" She's pointing at me. What an idiot. I'm not trying to flap my arms, it's how they fall when I jump.

It doesn't matter. Now I'm exhausted and sitting on the floor. I lay down on my back and stare at the ceiling. I kind of miss my Brenda ceiling fan…

My eyelids are so heavy. Stop fighting it. Then I hear a familiar voice, "Hey, May-May."

"Annie…" I let my eyes close.

I'm in the sky, a beautiful blue sky with puffy white clouds. I know I'm dreaming, but I'm hugging my daughter and I can actually feel her in my arms. There's Dave too. Oh, they're both glowing! I'm hugging him now. He passionately presses his lips against mine. I kiss him back and a tear rolls down my face. I want to stay here forever.

Then he's ripped away from me. He and Annie explode into a flock of white doves, then fade into mist over a mountain top. I scream, "Don't go! Take me with you!"

Someone has a hold of my arms and I'm being lifted into the air. I'm going with them, but then I'm shaken into consciousness.

I open my eyes, "Brenda? No! No, let me go! I have to go with them!"

"I'm getting you out of here. Let's go. One foot in front of the other."

My legs are weak and all I want to do is close my eyes and return to my family. We're stopped and seated at a small table. A nurse brings me a cup of lukewarm coffee, which I drink happily to wash down this awful taste I have in my mouth.

"I can't believe this," Brenda says, "How did you even get in here? You know, that old man was kissing you?"

Ah, of course the tear I so affectionately felt was only the old man's drool. Hm, I can't remember the last time I cried. Wait, yes I do. When I got the news about Annie tears streamed from my eyes for what seemed like forever, until one day they dried up.

Brend'as yelling at me now, in a stern whisper tone, so I think it's as good a time as any to try and cry. I close my eyes hard and contort my mouth—all of which hurts the gashes on my face. I take shallow breaths and strain letting each breath out, my face is hot. I whine a little too.

"It's okay. Let it out," she says while rubbing my back.

No tears come out, but it's effective at quieting her, so I try for another second or two... Nope, nothing. Oh well. I stand up and stretch then let my arms drop, my shoulders slump down, back hunched, and walk out of the room. My sister follows.

She must have brought her own car because we are standing at valet. While waiting, she turns to me,

"Well, things can only go up from here! At least you're rich!" I know she's trying to make light of everything now she's yelled at me. She's a glass half-full kind of person. I'm not a half-full or half-empty person. It's just a cup. It's just money.

CHAPTER THREE

Broken Unicorn

I'm sitting in a bath Brenda made for me, back at the house I used to call home when I had a family. She checks in on me every two minutes. I guess in her eyes I'm not above slipping under the water for too long.

I get out of the tub and don't bother drying myself off, the sheets will do that. I do a belly flop onto my bed. Ow. My face. I forgot about the glass table, the hospital, and all my butterfly bandages.

She lays out a pair of clean underwear, sweatpants and a sweatshirt on the bed in front of me, "Can you dress yourself okay?"

With my face still pressed into the messy covers I say, "Of course I can, don't be ridiculous."

"All right. I'll go make you lunch."

I can't imagine what it's going to be. Something awful, I'm sure.

She returns as I finish wrestling the sweatshirt over my bandaged head. I sit on the bed and she hands me a peanut butter and jelly sandwich. Pretty hard to mess that up, though she's heavy handed with the peanut butter and my tongue keeps sticking to the roof of my mouth.

Out of the corner of my eye I notice Brenda standing there, fidgeting with her hands. Ugh, she's annoying even when she's quiet. Since my mouth is full and I'm holding my sandwich with both hands, I stomp my foot on the ground to get her attention.

Finally, she says, "I have to tell you something."

Well, duh.

"During the months I didn't visit you, I had a lot of time to think." She sits next to me. "I had already lost my job so, I packed my things…" She waits for me to look her in the eyes and continues, "I'm moving in."

I clench my sandwich, shaking my head and screaming in my thoughts, but all I can muster is mumbled words through peanut butter, "No. No, you said you weren't coming back until I called you!"

"What can I say? I wanted to see how you would react, and your guarded response, 'good' showed me you need my help. Then your outburst and accident made me realize you need me *full time*. I think it would be best for both of us, and you obviously can't be trusted by yourself in your state."

In my state? I can't believe she's blaming me! I was perfectly capable until she came barging in. I fell while *in* her company, not alone. It's her fault! 'In my state' she

19

says. Unbelievable. I swallow the gob of peanut butter. "If you're moving in, then I'm leaving."

"Don't worry, I'm going to keep a close eye on you. We can heal together while living off the settlement for a while."

Shit. She's been planning this. I take another bite of the squished sandwich and pace around the room. I hear a large truck out front. I drop the sandwich and charge to the window. There's a freaking truck in my driveway with one of those huge portable storage units the size of a garage! This can't be happening. This can't be happening.

Now she's outside talking to the driver, gesturing for them to 'put it right here'. Right in the driveway. It's happening. It's freaking happening. Damn it, Brenda! I have to get out of here now or I might not get another chance. I run around the room trying to focus. Small travel bag from closet. Annie's letter. Small framed picture of me, Dave and Annie. Pajamas. Wallet with ID. I'm good. I'm good... I'm forgetting something... Bank card!

I run downstairs with my packed bag and rummage through the piles of papers in the kitchen to find my card. It has to be here somewhere.

"What are you doing?" She's caught me.

I shove the wallet in a pocket of my bag, hike up the sleeves of my sweatshirt and continue throwing papers around. She's trying to grab hold of my wrists, so I keep thrashing my arms around.

She yells, "Stop it, just stop!"

My arms are tired anyway so I drop them to my sides and yell back at her, "I can't do it. I won't do it. I cannot live with you!"

We stare at each other like our eyes are locked in a

battle of wills.

Then she pulls something from her back pocket, "Let me guess, you're looking for this?" She holds up my bank card.

I lunge for it.

She turns and runs upstairs into Annie's room.

"Not that room!" I scream.

She's in my baby girl's room that hasn't been touched since she left for camp. I barge in, "Get out! Get out of here you wretched woman!" I hurl myself at her and we tumble on the floor.

We wrestle, screaming at each other, our hands, elbows and feet flailing. I get myself on top of her and try to press her arms down to the floor. She thrusts her pelvis up and I fall over her. I'm clawing at her legs as she gets to her feet, then I jump up and slap her in the face. She has an expression I've never seen before, then her eyes narrow and she shoves me. Seriously? I stumble backward into Annie's night table but steady myself within a second, then turn around in time to watch, as if in slow motion, my baby girl's unicorn lamp falling down onto the rim of the trash can. The head breaks clean off.

I envision my sweet baby girl on the zip line and I fall to my knees on the floor. My hands are shaking as I gently pick up the unicorn head in one hand, the body in the other.

"Oh, May, I'm so sorry. I didn't mean—I thought her room would calm you down…"

I scream, "Get! Out!"

Shame and sorrow wash over her stupid face as she backs out of the room and shuts the door.

∞ • ∞

I need revenge. I've calmed down and shoved my emotions back into the depths of the emptiness in my heart, and now I'm listening at the door to figure out if Brenda's in the guest room, which I guess she thinks is her room now. The light in the hall turns off. The TV turns on. I wait a minute then slowly open the door and sneak out.

Down in the garage I find a roll of duct tape, but I need something to hold her still first. I find my pocket taser in the junk drawer in the kitchen that Dave had bought me. It's the kind you have to press against someone to zap them, so I'll have to be close and quick.

Creeping up to the guest bedroom door, I can see the light is still on in there. I wait and pick at the end of the duct tape to get it ready.

I'm tired of waiting. I burst into the room. She's laying in bed, so I fling myself onto her, taser zapping, eager for contact.

It works! Her body is spasming uncontrollably. I pull a length of tape, tear it with my teeth and hold it with my mouth while I wrestle her arms then tape her wrists together. She's stopped spasming now and is laying there motionless and breathing heavy. I move on to her ankles, holding them together with one hand, wrapping tape around and around with my other hand.

"Wha—" She coughs and stammers, but she can't seem to move her body yet. "What the hell are you doing!?"

Gah! I hate it when she shrieks like that. I press a length of tape over her mouth.

I take a few steps back. She sits up and starts bouncing up and down to scoot to the edge of the bed.

Now this is entertainment. I know she's not seriously hurt or anything. It was only a low voltage pocket taser. I'm grinning. Now she's fallen out of bed onto her stomach. She grunts then rolls over to sit and lean against the night table.

She yanks the tape off her mouth. "What the hell, May?"

Damn, I should have taped her fingers better. "Where is my bank card?"

"You know what? I thought you could never do anything so horrible, say anything so horrible, to push me away. But you've done it. All I've ever been is nice to you and—"

"You had this coming. Where is my bank card?"

She points with both hands to her purse. I grab my bank card out of it, and some cash and walk out. From the hall I hear her yell something about cutting her loose. I just did, in my own way. It's better this way. Now she can live her own life and I don't have to put up with her smothering me.

I grab my packed bag, slip on my old sneakers, and walk to the gas station a couple blocks away where I use their phone to call a cab. When the cab pulls up, the driver is staring at me. I don't smile or anything, because it hurts, everything hurts. I get into the backseat and hug my bag that has Annie's letter and my family picture inside.

"Uh…where you headed?" the cab driver asks as he hangs a little bird ornament from his rearview mirror.

I look out the window, up at the orange tinged sky, "Airport."

CHAPTER FOUR

Following The Magic

I used to love the airport, but now? I'm undecided. On the one hand I'm getting far away from Brenda, but on the other hand, I'm leaving all my memories behind and traveling alone. This is also the first time I've even been out of town since Dave passed.

I'm realizing I don't know who I am anymore. Daughter, wife, mother—I'm no longer any of those things. I'm just me again, but older and trapped in a body that's been stretched and scarred from bringing a child into this world, but I no longer have my child, my purpose. Would it have been better or worse to lose her as a baby like so many other mothers have lost babies? I mean, if there's such a thing as fate, and if one believes it's going to happen anyway, wouldn't sooner be better? I suppose either way I would still be alone.

Walking through the airport I'm awkwardly aware I'm not wearing a bra under this sweatshirt. Oh well. Who cares, right? Not me.

The sun is setting and I don't know where I'm headed yet, so I sit at the end of the bar, as far away from the other patrons as I can get. Does anyone work here? It's been so long since I've had a drink. I think I deserve one.

Ah, "Bartender!" Shit, that came out louder than I expected. At least it worked, here he comes.

He's about thirty years old judging by his face, but with salt and pepper hair, and he doesn't say a word. I guess he's waiting for *me* to speak while he dries a glass with a rag, like in movies.

I sit up straight. "I'll have a glass of your most expensive red wine." Since Brenda has pounded it into my head that I'm a millionaire now, I might as well treat myself every now and again.

"C'mon, lady, this is an airport."

I could slap that smug look right off his face. But, I won't risk being sent back to town now I've come this far. "Fine. A glass of whatever red you have. You do have wine, don't you?"

He pulls a standard, white labeled bottle and pours the smallest glass I've ever seen. "That'll be six dollars."

"I changed my mind." I need something stronger, but I don't know what to order, and this bartender is obviously not going to be any help.

He grumbles under his breath.

"Oh, give me a break. Can't you see what I've been through?" I point at my face.

"Fine."

"Fine!" I grab a menu but I can't focus. "Forget it, gimme that little glass of wine." I have to make a hefty decision soon, unless I set up camp in the airport and live here for a while. They do have a bathroom.

The loud-speaker blares, "Final boarding call for Flight 287 to Toronto."

Hmm… Canada? Nah, I'm sick of the cold. Sure it's not so bad here now, but it'll be snowing again soon. It's always around the corner.

I take a gulp of my wine. It's so tart one of my eyes is squinting uncontrollably, pulling my bruised and gashed skin. I finish it anyway and order another.

While waiting for my second order of wine, I hear a young girl somewhere behind me crying out, "Mommy? Mommy!"

I jump out of my seat and rush toward the sound. She has my Annie's voice when she was young, before she started calling me May-May.

My heart aches when I see her. While the child is the most beautiful mixed-race girl I've ever seen, she's not my baby girl. The part of me that holds on to a sliver of hope that my baby girl is going to walk around the corner falls back into numbness. If it were my daughter, I would want someone like me to help her, so I take the child's hand. She jerks it away from me.

I kneel down to her eye level. "It's okay sweetie, I'm going to help you." I smile even though it hurts.

The girl blinks her watery brown eyes and for a moment I do see Annie in her. I remember the time she thought she was lost in the grocery store, even though Dave and I were right behind the canned pineapple display. I should have told her we were hiding on purpose to see what she would do. I guess now I'll never get to.

The girl starts crying.

"Oh, it's okay. It's okay. What's your name, sweetheart?" I ask.

"P-Paisley,"

"Paisley? What a beautiful name. I'm going to be loud now, but everything is okay, I'm going to find your mommy."

She nods while rubbing her eyes.

While keeping a hold of the girl's hand, I stand up straight and yell, "Attention! Attention! Lost child!" My voice echoes down the hallways.

Only half the people in this dumpy airport even turned to look. Ridiculous.

An airport security officer approaches and tries to tell me he's got this from here. This? Oh, hell no. He probably meant this situation, but the way he said it, like the little girl was some lost purse rubbed me the wrong way.

"No. I'm staying with her. Back off and do your job. Use the loud-speaker."

"Ma'am, calm down, you're scaring the child." He turns his head and says something else into his official walkie-talkie. I'm pretty sure I heard the word crazy.

"*You* are scaring her. Go find her mommy!"

"Ma'am, let go of the child."

"What? No!" I hold Paisley tighter.

The officer steps closer. I move back with the little girl, and yell to the ceiling, "This child is missing her mommy!"

The officer yanks the girl from me while I'm yelling. Paisley is bawling now. Another officer arrives and stands between me and the girl and starts ushering me backward.

I clench my fists and plant my feet. "I'm just trying to help. What is with you people?"

Finally, a distressed woman runs over, calling out, "Paisley? Paisley?"

Then Paisley yells, "Mommy!"

Thankfully they are reunited, and in time to save me from being locked away in the loony bin again. Apparently I have a knack for it.

Now Paisley's mother is looking at me like some predator trying to steal her child so I tell her, "I promise you I was only trying to help. I would want someone to do the same for my Annie."

The mother pauses, then shakes my hand, "Thank you so much."

It's about damn time I got some credit. "You're very welcome."

Feeling good for once, I saunter past the officers with my bandaged head held high.

When I get back to my seat at the bar, my suitcase is still there, so that's good, and my second tiny glass of wine is waiting for me. I'm on an upswing. I gulp the wine and watch the mother and daughter meet up with a man who is obviously Paisley's father.

I'm proud of myself for doing a good deed.

Paisley screeches, "Disney World? Yay!"

Huh. What are the chances? The first time my Annie rode in a plane, Dave and I took her to Disney World. She was nine years old, her eyes full of wonderment, amazement, excitement. There isn't really one word to describe it, but I'll never forget it.

Come to think of it, that was her only plane ride because one year later Dave had his heart attack.

Afterwards, I never even took her out of town, or allowed her to go too far by herself, except the stupid camp with the stupid zip line. Maybe a part of me knew somehow…I can't think about it. I finish my drink.

The loud-speaker blares, "Flight ten thirty-one to Orlando is now boarding."

Ten thirty-one? Annie's birthday is October 31. Could this be a sign? And to Orlando of all places? Oh, what the hell, I've got nowhere else to go, might as well go where the magic is right?

I pay the bartender his twelve dollars, no tip. As it turns out I had enough of Brenda's cash leftover from the cab, so I didn't spend any of the settlement money.

At the ticket booth I say, "One ticket to Orlando, the one that's boarding now." I notice a hint of excitement in my own voice, but try not to pay attention to it. Happiness spooks easy these days.

The lady behind the counter clickety-clacks on the keyboard. "I'm sorry, ma'am, the next available flight to Orlando is tomorrow at noon."

Damn. I knew this upswing wouldn't last. Oh well. If the flight is booked, the flight is booked.

"Actually, you're in luck," she says, "there was a cancellation so we do have one seat available."

"I'll take it." Ugh. This purchase is definitely coming out of the settlement money.

On the plane, I spot Paisley with her parents, but I keep my back toward them as I get to my seat. I'm tired and want to sleep, but I also feel sick. It's not the altitude because the plane isn't even in the air yet. It's because I used some of the settlement money. I'm sure of it. Am I going to feel this way after every purchase? That my baby girl paid for this with her life? I didn't think all this traveling through, but I'm away from Brenda and hopefully this sickness will pass.

The plane takes off and the lights of the city I've lived in all my life get smaller and farther away in my window view. I look out at the twinkling stars one last time, then close the shade and then my eyes. No more Brenda. No more apologies from people who pity me. No more constant reminders of a life I no longer have. I'm off to find true solitude. If I'm lucky, and if there is a God, He'll take me to be with my family soon.

Normally I read Annie's letter to fall asleep, but I don't want to risk losing it. I clutch my bag on my lap and read it from my memory. I'm drifting to sleep and feeling better about using some of the money because maybe it's the only time I'll have to spend any of it. Perhaps I won't wake up. This would be a good ending for me, to die surrounded by happy families, and already halfway to Heaven.

CHAPTER FIVE

Not So Magical

Why? Why do I keep waking up? For what? I mosey through the terminal in the airport then find myself in what looks like the center of a mall. There's a fountain in the middle, surrounded by palm trees and benches and there's shops all around the perimeter. The ceiling is five stories up and each floor is lined with balconies—are those hotel rooms? Perfect! I need some time to think, maybe get some more sleep. The flight wasn't long, but I'm not a good napper, I want to sleep for more than three hours.

At the hotel counter there's pamphlets with real estate properties. I flip through one while waiting for the lady to get off the phone and address me. Home in a subdivision? No. Condo Villa? No. Apartment in the heart of Orlando? Hell no... Ah, here's one: Authentic Florida cracker house located off the beaten path; on the edge of the quaint town of Rise; on one acre of land right on the edge of beautiful freshwater marshland; only an hour drive from the airport. Forty-eight thousand dollars.

I try to picture it. Quiet sunrises, quiet sunsets, solitude. It's perfect. Probably too late to call on it now though. With my luck it's probably sold already. No way a property with that much land, listed at that price, is still available. If I call in the morning and it's still for sale, then maybe it's meant to be.

I interrupt the lady behind the counter, "Room for the night."

She gives me the finger. No, not that one, the one that's appropriate for public use. I sigh loudly and wait. She still hasn't even made eye contact. Rude. I don't even want a room now.

I sit on the side of a nearby bench so I can lay down on it, but before I could even set my bag down as my pillow, some younger woman sits next to me. She's talking on her cell phone while she adjusts her cleavage and surrounds herself with her designer luggage, taking up the rest of the space on the bench.

In my most pitiful tone, I say, "Excuse me."

She doesn't respond to me, but says into her phone: "Nobody, just some beat up old lady. Anyway, what was I saying? Oh, right, that chick in class is so gross! Like an ogre, yeah!" She laughs.

Seriously? "Excuse me!"

She jerks the phone away from her ear, "What!"

"Can you move to another bench? There's plenty."

"No. You move."

"I was here first and I want to lay down."

She talks into her phone, "God! This crazy old bitch is all up in my shit over here."

"What is wrong with you kids today? When I was young—"

She gives me the finger. Yeah, that one.

What a rude little snot! I kick one of her smaller bags and it flies several feet away.

She jumps up, "What is wrong with you psycho?"

Then, while her back is turned, I throw the rest of her luggage away from *my* bench and lay down across it so she can't sit back down. "It's called respect. If you don't give it, you won't get it."

"Screw you!" She stomps away.

Ahh, seniority wins. My family would be proud of me…I think about Annie's letter and my family picture in my bag under my head. My daughter never would have turned out like that.

For about thirty seconds I'm proud, but then it hits me, she will never get to be an adult. She'll never find love, have a career, have kids…all because I let her go to that stupid camp. If only I said no.

∞ ● ∞

I wake up with a crick in my neck, unsure of where I am. Then the loud speaker calls out a boarding flight and now I remember. An older man approaches me, hands me two dollars and says, "God bless you," then walks away before I can even clear my throat to tell him I'm not homeless. Well, I guess technically I am. I may own a house up north, but if you believe the saying, 'home is where the heart is' then my home is in Heaven…

stop thinking about it. Well, I might as well get a coffee with that man's money.

I sip my small cup of black coffee at the coffee bar as the people of the airport pass by. There's something about each person that reminds me of Annie or Dave or the life I used to have. The sooner I can get out of here the better. I finish my coffee on the way back to the hotel.

There's some middle-aged man taking all the real estate pamphlets. I hurry over. Before I can yell at him, his overwhelming but otherwise pleasant cologne hits the back of my throat and I cough.

"Oh, Good morning!" He extends his hand,"Luis Garcia with Sun-Rise Realty. Are you interested in a property?" His voice is lively with a noticeable Spanish accent, but I can understand him well enough. I'm not sure if I can handle his energy though.

I shake his hand. "The cracker. In Rise."

"Yes, forty-four Limpkin. That beauty is available."

Well, it's meant to be. "I'll take it. I can pay cash."

He squints his eyes, then smiles. "Really? Fantastic! I can definitely help you with that. When would you like to see it?"

"When I own it."

"Okay, but I do recommend you see it first, since a home is a big investment."

Does he want the sale or not? I can't believe this guy. "It's a house, I don't care what it looks like."

He doesn't say anything. What's his problem? I can't tell if he's thinking or judging me.

"I'm sorry, I have to ask. Are you all right?"

"Why?" Why would he ask that? Of course I'm not, but I just want him to sell me the freaking house.

"I mean," he touches his forehead then his cheek,

"were you in some kind of accident?"

Oh. Right. "Yeah. I'm fine."

"You're not running from the law or anything?" He laughs.

The law? He probably meant asylum. I'm pretty sure he's making a joke, but I'm getting tired of this. I snap, "I fell into a glass table. Does that somehow make me unfit to buy the house?"

"Oh, gosh, no. I'm so sorry. I didn't mean to offend you."

I stare at him.

He continues in a more cautious tone, "When can you come to do the paperwork? My office is actually in Rise, it's a lovely town, I live there myself."

"As soon as possible. I'm ready now."

"Okay, I can text you the address and meet—"

"I don't have a cell phone. Or a car." Because I left both up north in my haste to get away from Brenda, not that I was good at using either. "If you drive me then we can get this done and part ways." I'm a little remorseful for being short with him, but I'm here to *not* know anyone.

"Of course, I'd be happy to. Let me put these out..." He pulls a stack of new pamphlets from his briefcase and sets them on the counter, "Okay, now we can go."

Finally.

"Can I carry this for you?" He reaches for my bag.

"No!" I jerk it away from him. "I—I have some things that are precious to me in here."

"Okay. I understand... Um, my car is this way, it's a little bit of a walk."

"Fine."

We exit the airport and I swear it's like I walked into a giant sauna. I pull up the sleeves of my sweatshirt.

He stops at the smallest four-door car I've ever seen and says, "This is it." It has to be at least a decade old judging by the rust spots alone. Hope it has air conditioning.

The passenger door doesn't open, of course.

"Here, let me get that. It sticks sometimes." He bumps his hip into the door then opens it for me.

I get in and hold my bag on my lap. The inside is clean and smells like his cologne. Hell, I probably smell like his cologne from walking with him. Somebody should tell him not to wear so much.

Once he starts the car, he lets it idle while he blasts the air conditioning, which isn't even cold. Then he turns to me, "I just realized I don't know your name."

"May."

"Nice to officially meet you May. Have you had breakfast yet? I know I'm starving."

I doubt that, given the extra cushioning in his stomach area. I mean, he's not obese or anything, but he seems to eat well enough. Why do people say that anyway? There's people in third world countries actually starving. Ridiculous.

I'm a little hungry, but I want to get all this over with. If I'm going to get that sick feeling then I'd rather not buy myself one little breakfast out of the settlement money that I'll probably throw up anyway.

He says, "My treat."

Eh, it's a win-win situation. "Okay, yeah. Something quick though."

He flashes me a smile and starts driving. So. Slow. Like a teenager who's learning. I could walk faster, not that I would in this heat. Now I'm thinking about free food, I wish he would step on the gas. Of course, this piece of junk probably doesn't even go any faster since it's already squealing.

Only a few minutes later we arrive at this restaurant on wheels. Luis said it's called a Food Truck. Why would anyone want food made on a truck? Exhaust anyone? Some eggs with a side of motor oil?

He reaches for his keys to turn the car off, so I say, "No, keep it running."

"You don't want to pick something out?"

"It's too hot." I mean, hello? I'm wearing sweatpants and a sweatshirt in Florida.

He gets out and walks with a little skip in each step. While ordering our food, he's shifting his weight from hip to hip like he's dancing a salsa. Maybe he needs to use the restroom? What could he have to be so happy about? Probably the commission he's going to make off me buying that property.

He gets back in the car with two paper plates and hands me one. I'm not even sure where to start on this hot sandwich covered in powdered sugar with melted cheese oozing out of it. Looks good though. Maybe I'll have a heart attack like my Dave did and be reunited with my family and not have to deal with any of this.

"Hope you like ham and cheese Mallorca. It's delicious. I promise." He takes a bite out of his sandwich.

"What did you call me?" Sounded like May-orca. Did he just call me a whale?

"No. No. No. Mallorca." He points to the sandwich on my plate.

"Oh." I take a little bite. This is the best thing I've ever tasted! And now I kind of hate myself for enjoying this right now. This should be shared with the ones I love, but they'll never get to try it. I set the sandwich down on my plate.

"You don't like it?"

"No, I do, it's… the best thing I've eaten in a long time." I picture some of the worst under-cooked and over-cooked meals Brenda fed me. Good riddance.

He smiles then continues eating as he starts driving.

Well, Dave and Annie would want me to enjoy this, right? I eat it slow and savor each bite as though they can taste it too. Plus, the longer it takes me to eat, the less conversation I have to partake in with this guy.

Luis says, "So, do you have family coming down soon?" He keeps glancing at me so I shake my head. Hopefully he'll change the subject or better yet, stop talking altogether. I keep my face turned away from him.

He asks louder, "Any family?"

Did he not see me shake my head? What do I even say? Yes, but not anymore? No, but I used to? I'm not going to answer him.

A moment later we're at a stop light. "Are you sure you're okay?"

Ugh. He's starting to remind me of Brenda.

"I don't mean to pry, but I've seen enough grief to know what it looks like, so I hope I'm not being too forward by asking this: Did someone you love pass away? Just tell me if I'm wrong…"

The light turns green but he's still staring at me.

"Green light." I point at the stoplight.

He starts driving again.

After a bit of awkward silence, he says, "I'm very sorry for your loss. I lost my wife to cancer a few years ago, God rest her soul. Now I'm raising our three beautiful daughters on my own, which is difficult, but easy compared to losing my wife. That was the hardest thing I've ever had to go through."

This is depressing. I can't finish my sandwich now.

He continues, "Losing someone you love is life-changing, but I find it helps to focus on the blessings you still have in your life. I thank God every day for my daughters… How did you lose your loved one?"

First of all, I didn't lose them. They're not sitting in some lost and found bin waiting for me to retrieve them. Second of all, at least he still has his kids. What I wouldn't give to still have my Annie. She was the only reason I was able to function after losing Dave. It was only because of her I found a sense of peace with his passing, even though it still hurts. Without her, I'm lost.

"Have you talked to anyone about your feelings?"

Why would I want to talk about it? That doesn't do any good. It perpetuates the sadness. I'm better off not even thinking about it.

"What was your loved one's name?"

Huh, I can't remember the last time I said their names out loud. It's not that I want to answer him, it's more of a curiosity. And what could it hurt? I'm never going to see this guy again after this. "My husband's name is—was Dave. And my daughter…was…" I'm wrong. This hurts like hell. See? Talking about it makes it worse.

Luis gasps, "Oh, your husband *and* your daughter? I'm so sorry…It's good you can say their names. That's a step in the right direction and, you know, It's good to talk about these things so they don't eat you up inside."

Who is he to tell me what I have to do? He needs

to mind his own damn business and quit trying to get me to share. Oh, of course, I get it now, he's probably been going to some support group. Good for him and all, but I didn't sign up for therapy.

"I'm not crazy or anything, but I believe in fate. You lost your husband and daughter, and here I am with my daughters and I lost my wife. I think we were meant to cross paths, maybe so I could help you."

I don't need help. I need to be left alone.

He continues to yammer on, but I tune him out.

Finally, we pull up to a bright yellow building with the name Sun-Rise Realty and some palm trees painted on the front windows. Lets get this over with.

CHAPTER SIX

44 Limpkin

Inside Sun-Rise Realty there's a couple other people working on computers. All at once they look up at me. It's too small in here to be so brightly lit with fluorescent bulbs, all their faces are washed out and shiny. Poor people.

We go to Luis' office in the back where he sits behind the desk and I sit in one of the two swivel computer chairs on the other side. He's back to being the realtor instead of a wannabe therapist, which will hopefully speed this along. Plus, he says there's no real seller involved since the property is bank owned and apparently they've been trying to get rid of it for some time now.

He's reading me an inspection report made after the place was renovated up to code. "Would you like to have your own inspection done?"

"No." I swivel in my chair, stroking my bag on my lap with my thumbs.

A while later he hands me a small stack of papers. I pretend to read through it, then sign and initial where needed. I pull out my checkbook.

He says, "Usually we don't accept personal checks, but I guess I can make an exception for you if you can give me some assurance the funds are there."

"It's there, and plenty more."

He's silent, waiting for an explanation.

"Because of the wrongful death settlement—" my voice cracks and I clear my throat, "for my daughter..." Come on, May, hold it together.

"Oh, I'm so sorry." He places his hand over his heart. "How did it happen?"

Seriously? I can't believe this guy's nerve. "I don't want to talk about it. Is that enough 'assurance'? "

He pauses for a moment, then says, "Yes. I trust you."

I write out the check.

"Now we wait for the money to clear then we can meet to sign the final papers and I can give you the keys."

Excuse me, what? "I don't get them now?"

"I'm sorry, it's just part of the process."

I let out a long, loud sigh and lean back in my chair.

"I can take you to see it, if you want? It's right on the other side of town."

Spinning back and forth in my chair I glare at the lights on the ceiling. If only I could go to sleep and have the whole thing be done when I wake up so I can go back to sleep.

"Then I can drive you to a motel so you have a place to stay, and you can start shopping for furnishings."

Shopping? I'm starting to get that sick feeling now.

He leans forward on his desk.

I say, "Fine."

"Wonderful. Shall we?"

I guess we freaking shall.

∞ ● ∞

Back in his car, Luis is talking like a therapist again. He's using sincerely meant words that sound like Brenda and her constant pestering to 'focus on the good' and 'find the light in the darkness'. I can't stand it. Part of me wants to yell at him, but I don't.

Rise is a small town all right, but there appears to be a little bit of everything you'd find in a more modern city. There's the one main road we're on now, with strips of grass between the sidewalks and the buildings, even a few trees. The streets running off the main road have a mix of more little shops and small houses. Not too many people walking around either, so that's good.

Luis is pointing out his recommendations on places to eat, historical facts about different buildings, then he points to a street on the right, "My house is down there."

Now I tune him out. I don't care where he lives.

A few minutes later, the town is behind us and the road is lined with a natural overgrowth of trees, bushes and vines, like development just stopped. It's a little creepy actually. There could be dead bodies, half-eaten by who knows what kind of creature, right inside the brush.

Once we go around a couple of curves, there's a small dirt road on the right, partially hidden by overgrowth. On the corner is an old wooden mailbox, and hanging from it is a piece of wood with '44 Limpkin' burned into it.

The driveway actually opens wide with grass on either side separating the dirt from the forested area, which makes the creepiness drop way down. It's quite nice back here. I can't see the house yet because the driveway is long and curves to the right.

Just past the curve, the forest stops on the left and the marsh is revealed. A vast area of flat land with shimmering water between tall grasses and reeds. There's a tree line in the distance with a huge clear blue sky above.

Pulling up to the house, I can hardly believe my eyes, there's such a strange mix of beautiful and dumpy. It's far enough away from the marsh to have solid land all around that's all dirt with patches of grass except one ancient oak tree to the left of the driveway, several feet in front of the house. To the right of the house is more forest. Nice and secluded. Good.

The house itself is constructed almost entirely of wood panels that have never been painted, and raised about a foot off the ground. There's a nice sized porch that runs the length of the front.

I open my door and have my foot on the ground before the car stops. Then I get out, close my eyes and listen. It's as quiet as I hoped other than the continuous buzzing of insects, but I'm okay with that.

Luis pipes in, "Fun little fact for you: limpkin is a type of bird. They love the marshes because they eat the apple snails that are all over the place."

I'm not really paying attention because I'm walking up three wooden steps onto the porch, whispering to myself, "Don't fall through. Don't fall through."

It's more sturdy than it looks. Nice breeze up here too. Aw, great view of the marsh from here with the oak tree on the left, very picturesque. I hope the sun sets over there.

As he's getting the key out to open the door he continues, "There's a lot of them around here, so you'll be sure to see them, hear them too. Limpkins are also known as Crying Birds."

Great, just what I need.

Inside the place is empty. Bare bones. It has an odd odor of lumber, cigar smoke and a stagnant pond maybe? I can't put my finger on it. Filtered sunlight is shining in through the windows illuminating floating dust particles and small flying insects.

"Don't worry, the birds are pretty quiet except at night and in the morning, and during mating season. There's not as many around here any more, so the noise shouldn't be too bad."

"When's mating season?"

"Oh, I'm not sure. Probably spring? Summer? Would you like to see the master bedroom?"

"Isn't it summer now?"

Luis chuckles. He must think I'm making a joke.

I wait with a straight face.

"Um, it feels like summer most of the year here, but it's technically fall."

Squinting my eyes at him, I continue to wait for a more specific answer.

"It's October."

Damn it. That means Annie's birthday is coming up. My stomach knots up as I picture her laughing, dressed in her fairy costume, surrounded by torn wrapping paper. I'd have had my closet full of gifts for her by now.

My head is throbbing. I sit down on the floor in the middle of the living space.

"So, as you can see, the place needs to be furnished. But it has been modernized for central air conditioning, plumbing, electric and telephone, all the while keeping the charm" Luis turns to face me, "Are you okay?"

I sigh then get up and head to his car.

He follows, "Lets get you checked into the motel in town for now so you can rest, and this weekend I'm going shopping with you, to help you furnish your new home, if that's okay? I would go with you sooner but I have to provide for my daughters."

This is not my home! It's a freaking old roof over my head. I get in the car.

He speaks occasionally during the drive but I keep my gaze fixed out the window, letting the trees blur together into one long splash of green.

We arrive at the one motel in this small town. It has ten rooms, and they're all available. Ugh, I have to use my bank card. I can't keep doing this. Maybe I'll get used to this feeling and eventually stop thinking about how my baby girl died for whatever I buy…probably not though.

He walks me to my room. "I'll pick you up at about ten Saturday morning."

I nod then shut myself inside and lean my back against the door.

The room has wood paneling all around, mustard color coverlet on the bed, and a small table with two chairs by the only window, which is framed with thick wool curtains. No ceiling fan.

I shuffle over to a giant brass lamp with an oversized lampshade and turn it on, then I step over to the window. Luis is getting into his car. I close the curtains. The room is now saturated in the dim yellow light from the lamp.

I set my bag on the bed and unpack Annie's letter, my little family picture and my pajamas. Then I strip off my sweatpants and sweatshirt and take a shower. The cool water cascades down my body and one by one the butterfly bandages slide off my face and get sucked down the drain.

CHAPTER SEVEN

Assurance

A pounding on the door in a musical pattern wakes me.

"Go away, Brenda!" I yell and roll over putting my back to the door.

"Good morning, May! It's Luis. Are you ready for your shopping day?"

Oh, right, I remember now. "No." I know I need stuff for the house and at least if I go with him then I won't have to pay for a cab on top of everything else. But I wish I had a magic wand. Of course, I would use it to bring my family back and be done with all of this.

"Okay, okay, no problem! I'm going to go and pick up some bagels and coffee and I'll come back in about twenty minutes, okay? Okay."

I stare at the clock on the wall.

Fifteen minutes later, I'm still in bed. The second hand of the wall clock is ticking along without a care in the world.

A car pulls up and judging by the squealing it's Luis and he's letting his car idle. Four minutes later the engine cuts off. Now I'll get out of bed.

Ew, my clothes from yesterday stink. It's funny how I don't notice the smell that comes with not changing, but I do notice when it comes to putting old clothes back on. Brenda would have called this progress. She usually washed my clothes so I didn't have the option of wearing old ones.

Whatever, my pajamas are comfortable. This won't be the first time I've been out in public in them. I comb my fingers through my hair, grab my wallet, then open the door. He's standing there, smiling wide, holding a paper bag and two steaming coffees in a cardboard drink carrier. "Good morning! Oh, I'm sorry, you're not dressed yet. I'll wait in the car, and you come out whenever you're ready."

This is going to be a long day. "I don't have anything else. Lets go." I take a coffee from him and start walking.

"Why the long face? Aren't you glad to be shopping?"

He's lucky he's not Brenda. I don't know him well enough to throw my coffee at him. Plus, he's my only ride and I still have to get the keys to my place. Guess I have to put up with him for... hmm, how long does it take for a check to clear?

He continues, "It'll be fun and painless I will make

sure of it! But, before we get you some clothes, our first stop should be the Pick & Patch, it's right on the way. They'll patch up your face and you can even pick up a piece of produce if you want, maybe a nice rrrripe banana, huh?" He rolls the R so long he sounds like a cat purring.

Remembering what my face looked like the last time I saw it, I nod. I can't believe their walk-in medical center also sells produce.

I eat my bagel and drink my coffee in the car and finish them both by the time we arrive at the Pick & Patch. It's in a small strip of stores and the first P is missing from their sign, so it reads: ick & Patch.

I'm patched up by a woman missing more teeth than she has in her mouth, so I decide I will treat myself to a piece of produce: an apple. It's been a while since I've had one and it makes me kind of thankful I have teeth. Not so thankful to have more butterfly bandages, though. Heal already! My face is so tight it's a struggle to take a bite out of my apple.

Luis leads me across the street to a little independent clothing store. It's so hot outside! The store better have shorts and tank tops. Maybe I'll get a bathing suit so I can properly swim in my own sweat. Disgusting.

There's no way I can finish this apple. It hurts too much. I drop it on the ground by a small tree between the street and the sidewalk in front of the shop so a squirrel can have it.

Even though I don't know what style of clothing is in fashion now, I know this store doesn't carry it. Everything has been embroidered, bejeweled, or has patches of flowers. Oh well, I grab a few pairs of shorts in different sizes and some tank tops then change in the bathroom/fitting room.

When I come out I'm holding my pajamas and all the clothes that fit in one arm, and the ones that didn't fit in my other arm. I'm now dressed in my new society approved clothes. Luis applauds. Maybe he's seeing something different? I look down at myself. Nope. I feel ridiculous. Here I am, May Flower Johnson, dressed in jean shorts with brightly colored flower patches on them and a tank top with a flower design made out of jewels covering my whole chest. Eh, the clothes fit, so who cares.

Luis is holding some new pajamas and a purple velvet track suit, which is apparently the fancy term for pants that are nicer than sweat pants but still stretchy like pajamas, and a matching jacket. It's perfect for me actually, since for some reason track suits are acceptable to wear in public and pajamas are not. He holds them up for my approval, "I thought you might like this."

I nod and grab a pair of flip flops too.

At the checkout counter, I hold my bank card, staring at it.

The giggly store owner plucks it from me with a smile, then says, "You look lovely dear, and," she leans closer to me and whispers, "in case you were wonderin', they sell razors next door."

What's that supposed to mean? You look lovely but you might want to go ahead and off yourself? Thinking about this takes my mind off the purchase for a minute. Then, when she hands me the receipt a small wave of nausea washes over me. I can't take this. I cannot handle this and I absolutely cannot handle shopping all freaking day!

Back in the car I turn to Luis, "That's it for me. I can't do it."

"Oh, but we still need to get you some furniture and—"

"I said I can't do it!"

There's a moment of silence. I lean over and put my head to my knees and realize what the store owner meant. My leg hair is so long it's soft instead of prickly. I rub my hands over my calves and shins. It reminds me of Dave and how we used to watch movies on the couch, sitting at opposite ends with our legs intertwined. He would laugh at my stubble, while I would pet his hairy legs as if we had a cat.

He softly says, "I didn't know this would be difficult for you."

"Well, it is! I told you the only reason I have any of this money is because of my daughters death! I can't take it!"

"I'm sorry…"

I take a deep breath as my thoughts reel around. There has to be another way to get the house livable. I need at least a mattress. A refrigerator would be useful too. Ugh. I shouldn't have bought that stupid house when I could have stayed in the shitty motel.

"Take me back to the motel."

He starts driving as if I commanded him to.

After a while he says, "You know…I could take care of furnishing your house for you. If you want?"

"What good would that do? It's the same thing." I'd still be spending the money and feeling sick.

"If you were to withdraw the cash, I could handle the shopping for you. You can tell me what you want and I'll go get it. That way you don't have to be a part of every single purchase. And I'm honest, you know I am. I'll save all the receipts."

Hm. He has a point actually, to get it all done in one shot. But why would he do that? Probably to run off with the cash.

He pulls over and parks on the side of the road then turns to me, placing his hand on mine, "I'm happy to help, really. I think what you are going through is much worse than the nightmare I went through because you're here by yourself…so let me be your support."

I'm thinking.

He continues, "I'll give you something to hold onto for assurance. I don't have much, but you could hold on to my wife's ring, which was my grandmother's," He pulls the chain around his neck and out pops a ring from under his shirt that has a ruby surrounded by diamonds. "This has been in my family for generations."

An heirloom? He'd hand over his dead wife's wedding ring?

"It's very dear to me though, so you'd have to promise to keep it safe…I've been where you are, and I know it's not easy. Accepting help is sometimes the hardest part…"

Great, here he goes again with the therapy talk. "Fine. Yes, I'll keep it safe. How much money will it take?"

"Well, you need appliances and basic furniture at least. Do you want new or used?"

"I don't care. Nicer mattress though."

"Okay. Two thousand dollars should be more than enough, and I'll give you what's left over. I'll get it done as quick as possible for you, but I'm juggling a couple of jobs and my kids. Are you okay staying in the motel for a while?"

"Fine."

He drives to the bank and I practically hyperventilate to work up the nerve to go in. I'm expecting the worst feeling yet. Writing the check for the house was easy in comparison. This is cash in hand.

I go in and withdraw the money. The teller puts the money in two envelopes which makes it a little easier because I'm not touching the cash directly. I run back to the car and flop into the passenger seat. My hands are shaking as I hand it over.

/

CHAPTER EIGHT

Signs

I haven't left my motel room since Luis dropped me off after giving him the cash a week ago. Or has it been two weeks? Three? Hm, I wasn't bothered by the motel room until I thought about how long I've been here. What's taking him so long?

He had stopped by real quick, a few days after, to tell me the money for the house cleared, and he gave me one key. I agreed he should hold onto the other key so he could work on the house without me having to open it for him since I truly own it now.

I haven't heard from him since then though. He's probably squatting in my house, living off my money. I'm such an idiot. But then why did he give me one key? Ugh.

I'm confused.

Then I remember he gave me that heirloom ring. Where did I put it? Oh, right, *he* put it in the small zipper pocket in my travel bag. Okay, so he should be coming back eventually, unless it was all a lie and the ring is worthless. He probably saw 'sucker' written all over my face. But he seemed so sincere…

Sitting at the little table, I'm staring out the window of my motel room and, as if I had called him telepathically, Luis pulls up and parks. My shoulders relax.

I pack my bag, then gently tuck Annie's letter and my little framed family picture inside. One last look around the room to make sure I didn't forget anything and I slip on my flip flops, turn off the lamp, leave the room and close the door behind me. I won't miss it, that's for sure.

His car is smoking from the muffler and all the windows are down. He gets out and leans on his open door, "Hey, look at you! You're healing up nicely."

I hadn't even thought about my face. The pain and tightness are all gone, and now I remember peeling off the bandages I got from the Pick & Patch because all the cuts had closed up. They're still noticeable though.

"You are going to be one happy lady!"

Doubtful. "Was there enough money?" I ask, making my way to the passenger side.

"Oh, yes. No problem." Luis gets back in the car.

I flop into the passenger seat, "What happened to the A/C?"

"Oh, I need to get it fixed again. It's okay, we have a nice breeze today."

Where? There's less humidity, but it's still too hot

to not have air conditioning.

A little voice from the backseat says, "Hi, May."

I jump and clutch my chest with one hand, my bag with the other, then spin around. Three beautiful little girls with dark hair and doe eyes that show a hint of the sadness I know all too well.

"We're sorry about your family," they say, almost in unison.

I work up a smile so they don't feel bad for scaring me, then turn back around in my seat and stare out the window.

Luis says to me, "I had to explain a little bit of your situation so they would understand why they had to spend extra time at their aunt's house."

"It's fine." But it's not. I'm down here trying to find solitude. I can't have him blabbing my story to anyone, even his daughters. They might tell their friends, who tell their parents, who tell their friends, then before I know it I'm surrounded by people trying to get an extra star sticker on their good-deed checklist.

He says, "Let me introduce you: Isabella is my oldest, in the middle is Sofia, and the little cupcake is Zoe."

I raise one hand and wave to them behind me, without looking.

Then he hands me one of the little paper money envelopes I had gotten at the bank. "This is what was left, just over two-hundred dollars, and the receipts are in there too. I hope you like how I fixed up your new home, and I'm sorry it took so long."

Damn it, it's not a home. I wish he'd quit calling it that.

"The ring?" he asks.

Oh, right. I open a zipper pocket on my bag and reach my hand in. Where did it go? It was right here, I saw him put it here. Shit, shit, shit. I frantically press my fingertips into each corner of the pocket, over and over again.

He asks, "Did you move it?"

"No! I swear, I didn't touch it, and I didn't go anywhere."

He turns my bag over, opens a smaller zipper pocket and pulls out the ring. Whew! I would've felt terrible if I lost it. Then he hands me a key on a Sun-Rise Realty keychain, "Here's the other key to your house. Congratulations again."

I nod.

One of the girls says, "Daddy, I'm hungry."

Luis responds, "I know, baby, we'll stop and get you some chicken nuggets after we drop May off, okay?"

Another girl says, "We had chicken nuggets yesterday."

How pitiful! Can't he afford something better to feed them? "Did you pay yourself?"

"Oh, no, it's my gift to you."

He's too nice. That's probably why he's in such a crappy financial position. I hold out the envelope, "Keep this at least." Even though I haven't seen if he's even done a good job at the house or not, two hundred bucks for weeks of work is not enough. He's got three daughters to provide for on his own.

"I can't take it."

"Why not? Did you get everything I'll need?"

"Well, yes. I got all of it, plus some food and decor, which I hope you like. You mentioned a nicer mattress, so I made sure to get a new, plush one, with the protective cover the store recommended, two deluxe pillows and two sheet sets, one lavender and one blue. I painted too, then burned some candles which made it smell better."

"Then it's settled." I stick the money in the glove compartment. Just making the place smell better is worth two hundred in my opinion. Plus the mattress? He deserves more.

A warmth washes over me, and at the same time I notice a huge yellow butterfly soar past the windshield. Is that a sign from my family? Am I supposed to give this family more? How much more? Annie?

Luis starts driving while I continue to try using my thoughts to communicate with my daughter in Heaven. She doesn't answer me in words, but a glare of sunlight catches my eye from a used car lot, so I believe it's an answer. A new car would be perfect for them.

"Pull in here." I'm almost excited. There's an energy surging through my body, like I'm inspired. Yes, that's it. I'm being guided by my loved ones and maybe I still have a purpose. Plus, I can get a car for myself so I can get around without having to pay a cab or depend on anyone.

I carry my bag with me as I walk into the dinky little building. A salesman, unshaven yet well dressed, approaches me, "Can I help you, ma'am?" He has a strong southern accent, unlike anything I've heard in Florida so far. He's either the first native I've met, or he's from some other south.

"See that man and his daughters out there? I want to buy them a mini-van. I want to buy myself a car too."

"All right. What'ya lookin' for?"

Seriously? I just told him. "A mini-van. And a car. Lowest mileage on the lot."

"Well, far as minivan's go, that white one out there that they're lookin' at is the best we got right now. We put it on the lot today, and it's only got fourteen thousand miles on it. It's about ten years old, but hardly used at all, as you can see, the paint's still good 'cause it was garage-kept."

"Price?"

"So, first, let me say that we aint yer typical used lot. We are family run and like to give the best deals we can to help out folks who can only afford used, while still makin' a livin' for ourselves, ya know?"

"Okay. So, what's the price." Now I'm thinking it's probably outrageous.

"Sixty-eight hundred."

That's a great deal! I think. Dave used to handle all this. I look around me for some sort of sign. There's a chip bag in the trash, he loved chips! Could that be a sign?

"I'll take it. And a car?"

He points to a run-down little silver car, "That one there's about the same situation, but wasn't stored too well. Some kids used it as a playhouse in the yard or somethin.'"

I refuse to be punished for my good deed, as the saying goes. "What else ya got?" Oops. I accidentally mimic his accent. Hope he doesn't notice.

"Well, that red one's got—"

Red? I don't even hear what he's saying because I'm lost in this tinge of excitement. It's a sporty sedan. Red was one of Annie's favorite colors. "I'll take it."

"Aint you gonna haggle me none?"

Oh, I forgot about that. "Yeah, I'm gonna haggle you." How do I do that?

We move over to his little desk and he pulls up the

van's information on the computer.

"I'd like it for six thousand instead. You should give me a deal because I'm buying two vehicles today."

"You payin' cash?"

"Check."

"All right, I can go as low as sixty-two hundred on the van."

"Okay!" Dave was six feet and two inches tall. Another sign! This is amazing.

Then he pulls up the red car's information on the computer. It's listed for almost nine thousand dollars, with just over sixty thousand miles.

"I want that one for seven thousand."

"You sure you got the funds for all this?"

"If you do seven—or six. Do six and I have it." I'm getting kind of confused with all these numbers, but I'm still pleased with myself. This is the first time I've haggled. Who knows if I'm doing it right. Dave would know.

"I gotta verify with yer bank."

"That's fine. So, you'll do six for the car?"

"Yeah, okay. It's been here for a while, and you seem serious about buyin' both."

"Oh, and the air conditioning works, right?"

"Yes, ma'am, everything is up to par on all our vehicles, lest we say otherwise. The car's got some stains and such inside, but that's just cosmetic. Had our mechanic go over 'em real good like he does every car on the lot."

I tell him my bank and he looks up the number for me to call. I give a teller access to my information, then hand the phone over for the salesman to talk numbers.

He hangs up the phone, "Ma'am, yer cleared to

write a check for these two vehicles, plus the fees for yer tags and what not."

I write the check for the total amount then go outside with the keys and paperwork. The salesman follows me with the temporary tags. We approach the white van where Luis and his daughters are still loitering.

The salesman goes around to the back of the van to put the temporary tag on. I'm smiling effortlessly for once as I get inside the van and turn it on, then test the air conditioning. It's nice and cold. I peer out the front windshield, waiting for another butterfly to cross my path. Nothing.

Luis stands by the open driver's side door with his daughters, "Did you buy this one, May?"

"I did."

"It's a nice vehicle, a great deal too. I would have bought this one myself if I could. One day."

"Well," I turn to him, "you just did!" I hand him the paperwork, "I got you a temporary tag for now until you decide what you want to do with your old car."

He's frozen, his mouth gaping.

I jump out of the driver's seat and nudge him to get in. He stumbles at first, then settles into the seat, feeling the steering wheel and adjusting the rearview mirror. I check the sky for a sign from my family that I'm doing a good thing. Still nothing.

"This is too much. I can't possibly—"

"I already bought it, so you can't refuse." I search the ground for anything that could be a sign. Part of me wants to have 'good job' written in the dirt, but there's only rocks.

"But what about you?"

I turn and point, "I bought that red one." Oh!

Maybe there's a sign waiting for me over there.

Isabella says, "Is this ours, Daddy?"

Sofia says, "Is it? Can we get in? Can we?"

He stammers then agrees.

The girls slide open the side door then pile inside, giggling and smiling. Now the salesman is ready to put my temporary tag on my new, used car, so I walk away with him.

Before I can get my car door open, the squeals of Luis' daughters are upon me.

Luis yells, "Group hug!" and they all latch on to me like I walked into some kind of giant human spider web.

Group hugs are one of those things that sound nice, but are kind of uncomfortable. Where do I put my hands? "Okay, okay, enough," I pry them off me.

"Thank you. Truly." Luis says with teary eyes. "You have no idea how much this means to me—to us."

"Well, you deserve it."

"I can't thank you enough!" He throws his arms around me. "You're an angel."

"It's okay. Come on, now."

He pulls away from me, wipes his eyes and clears his throat. "If there is anything you ever need, call me, and I'll be there for you." He hands me a few of his business cards, then turns to his daughters and says, "Girls, say thank you."

Isabella says, "Thank you, May."

Sofia says, "Thank you so much!"

Zoe utters, "Thanks M—May"

My attention snaps to Zoe. Did she call me May-May? Did my Annie speak through her? Damn it, I wanted another sign to make me feel good, but I just feel kind of sad.

Luis says, "Thanks again, and I mean it, if you need anything, call me!" Then he turns to his kids, "Okay, girls! I'll race you to our new van!" and they all run off together.

Watching them together makes me painfully aware of the holes in my heart. At least this is the last time I'll have to see them. But it's not fair! I don't want anymore stupid signs, I want my family back.

I slump into the driver's seat of my car and grip the steering wheel so tight my knuckles turn white as I hold back tears. Then a wet pile of bird poop splatters on my windshield.

CHAPTER NINE

Soft Kitty

Driving through town is a nightmare. Not because it's busy or anything, but because I can't get my eyes to quit tearing up. A stoplight turns yellow as I approach it and I have to slam on the breaks. "Ugh!" I scream and slap the palms of my hands on the steering wheel a few times, then grip it and scream again. Stupid car.

There's a bank on my right. Might as well get some more freaking money, because, why the hell not? Apparently I'm going to feel shitty no matter what I do. I withdraw a couple hundred dollars from the drive-up ATM.

Driving around the block I see a bar named Pinky's. It's a whole corner section of a long building that has other smaller shops and businesses. Bars must be a popular thing no matter where you are. I could use a drink. Thunder rumbles in the sky as I park. I grab my bag and hurry inside.

The place is roomier inside than it looked, and nicer than I thought it would be. It has soft lighting, beautiful woodwork and music that's not too loud. They have neon-lighted signs on almost every wall in between giant collages of memorabilia and posters, pool tables in the back, even a stage on the far side of all the tables. There's a few people milling around for happy hour, which I guess is typical. Dave and I were only occasional drinkers, but we watched plenty of movies.

I sit at the bar in the middle of the bar with my bag and wonder why they couldn't think of a different name for the bar. So stupid.

The bartender asks, "Getcha somethin', darlin'?" He's a burly man in a leather vest and pants.

"Do you have any bottles of red wine I can buy?"

"Sure. Merlot? Cabernet? And how many?"

"Um…a case of Merlot."

"Rough day?"

I nod. "Do you sell food too?"

He hands me a menu, but I don't want to read it so I hand it back, "What's good?"

"Can't go wrong with chicken tenders and fries."

"I'll take five orders to go."

He cocks his head. "It'll take a few minutes. Glass of wine while you wait?"

"Yeah, ok." One glass can't make me drive any worse. Of course, anyone who doesn't know where they're going is a bad driver. That reminds me, "Do you have a map of the town I can have?"

He pours my wine, "Where are you headed?"

"A house by the marsh, um…" Shoot, I forgot the address.

"Forty-four Limpkin?"

"Yes!" Wait. "How did you know?"

"It's a small town and I'm a bartender, I know everything." He winks.

Great.

He produces a map, then he takes a pen and draws two circles, "This is Pinky's, where you are now, and this is the house. Now you can always find your way back here too." He winks again then disappears behind a swinging door in the back, which I assume leads to the kitchen.

I'm tracing the route on the map with my finger, from circle to circle, when I feel a hand on my right thigh.

"Hey there soft kitty." Says a low woman's voice in my right ear.

I jump, smack her arm, then glare at her. The woman appears to be in her forties, has short brown hair spiked up with gel and is wearing a white tank top and a necklace with some claw or tooth about two inches long. At first glance I thought she was a man.

She leans her elbow on the bar, smoothly, "Saw you come in. Had to say hello."

I glare harder at her.

"I dig it, you know, the hair."

Are you freaking kidding me? Oh, right, I still haven't shaved my legs.

"I'm Deanna, what's your name?"

"Go away."

"Ooh, sassy too."

I move myself and my bag down a few barstools

and turn my back to her.

She appears in front of me.

I shout "What? What do you want?"

"Hey, hey. Shh, it's okay. I'm sorry. Wrong approach." She clears her throat. "Honestly, I'm nervous. I'm just getting back into the dating game. Also, you left your map and your drink."

"I'm not a lesbian," I snatch my map and turn away from her.

"Sorry, okay? Can I just talk to you for a minute?"

I turn and open my mouth to respond but then she says, "Lets start over. Hi, I'm Deanna." She sits on the barstool next to me.

"I don't feel like talking." I take my glass from in front of her and sip on it.

"That's okay, I love a good listener. So, I'm getting out of a bad breakup. She stole my car and…"

I find myself actually listening, even nodding along like I'm in one of those bar scenes in a movie. This is too bizarre. What kind of person starts spewing their drama on a stranger?

"…So then after I poured my heart out she told me she married that other chick already! Married her! Unbelievable, right?"

I nod.

"Whew, that felt so good to get it all out."

I raise my glass to gesture you're welcome, then take a gulp.

She's staring at me. "You're beautiful."

"Ha!"

"No, really, I mean it."

She doesn't get it. I don't care what I look like or who thinks I'm beautiful or not, I'm laughing because this whole situation is bonkers. Where are my chicken tenders? I finish my drink.

"Can I buy you another?"

"No."

Ah, here comes the bartender with my case of wine. Fancy Feathers? What an odd name. The picture beneath the name is eye-catching though. It's an outline of a person dancing, drawn in black ink on a white background, wearing a rainbow colored feathered boa. Hope it tastes as good as the art.

Oh, good, all my food is stacked in one large plastic bag. I check my pockets, then my travel bag for the cash I got from the bank, but I must have left it in the glove compartment of my car. At least I hope that's where it is and not on the ground in the parking lot. That same uneasiness is creeping into the pit of my stomach as I search now for my wallet. I'll have to use my bank card.

Deanna says to the bartender, "Hey, Chuck. How's it goin'?"

He says, "You're not bothering the patrons again are you? What did I tell you? I like you, I think you're a good person, but you've got to get over that drama with your ex. That was, what, three months ago?"

"Four. But, yeah, you're right, you're right."

As I hold out my bank card to the bartender, Deanna snatches it, "May? What a pretty name." Then she hands my card to the bartender.

I snap at her, "You know what? You don't do that. No normal person does any of *this*." I move my hands around to emphasize 'this'.

"What? Sit in a bar and have a conversation? Or are you homophobic?"

I look to the bartender for support, but clearly he's

waiting for an answer too. "This has nothing to do with gay people. There's nice gay people, and there's weirdos. There's nice straight people, and there's weirdos. Same with every type and color."

The bartender is nodding and laughing.

Deanna says, "So...I'm a weirdo?"

"Yes."

"Pfft. And you're not? With your hairy ass legs? Your scarred up face? Bitch, please."

Maybe she's right. I've definitely had my moments. "I mean, you're *acting* weird right now. I don't know you, so I can't judge for any time but now."

She's quiet as I'm putting my wallet away and trying to figure out how I'm going to get my bag, all my food and my case of wine out to my car.

"I'm sorry— Again." She picks up my case like it weighs nothing. "Can I help carry your stuff? I promise I'll be 'normal.'"

The bartender adds, "She's harmless. I've known her for years. Just a little lonely right now."

"Fine."

Deanna and I walk out to my car and load the back seat.

As I'm getting in the driver's seat, she's standing in front of the car, smiling, "Call me sometime so we can hang out."

I ignore her and drive off.

The sun is starting to set as I'm navigating to my new house. It didn't even rain. All that thunder and not a drop. Maybe it all evaporated before it hit the ground?

My driveway is so spooky in the dark. I park as close to the house as I can and leave my headlights on to illuminate the front yard and porch.

I'm kind of scared to get out of the car. Darkness has never bothered me, but a pitch black bedroom is totally different from the wilderness. Well, I can't sleep in my car... Or can I? No. I want to sleep on the nice mattress Luis said he bought me.

I jump out with my travel bag in one hand and my key in the other and start running. My sandals flap around. One flies off, I almost trip, then finally I make it up onto the porch. The headlights are behind me so my body is making a shadow over the lock and I can't see where to put the key in. The hairs on the back of my neck stand on end. I feel like something is going to scurry over and claw me to death any second now.

Found it! I practically fall inside, then slam the door shut so no critters sneak in. I set my stuff down then find a switch on the wall that turns the porch light on.

Damn it. I still have to go out and get my food and wine.

I run out, jump in the driver's seat, and turn off the car and headlights. The nighttime sounds of nature come roaring into my head. Oh, shit. What was that? Was that a hiss? Better not be a snake, I hate snakes.

Listening for a moment I figure it must've been my imagination because all I hear now is the incessant buzzing and chirping of insects and the pulsing croaks of toads. God, how could I be so stupid? There's no solitude here.

"Come on, May. You can do this. Grab the stuff and get inside." I whisper to myself, then jump out, open the door to the backseat, slide my arm through the handle of my food bag, then grab my case of wine with both hands. I grunt to lift it then stumble backwards, pivot and try to bump the door with my butt to close it. It barely moves but I don't care, I've gained forward momentum.

There's that noise again! I freeze, almost halfway to the house, and listen. A pair of glowing eyes near the ground grab my attention to the left of me where the marsh is. What the hell is that!

The eyes move closer to me then stop. My heart is pounding in my chest. Where do I go? I'll never make it to the house.

I step backwards and the eyes move closer again. Screw this. I drop the case and dive into the backseat of my car and pull the door shut. I'm safe, but I'm also trapped. This sucks.

A few minutes go by and I haven't been attacked, so I climb into the front seat and turn on the headlights.

Are you freaking kidding me right now? Is that a freaking alligator!? Of course it is. I press and hold the car horn and scream, "Go away!" but it actually comes closer.

Fine. Just fine. I lock the doors, turn the car on and get the air conditioning going. Lightning flashes in the sky, then thunder rumbles so loud my bones are vibrating. Now it's raining. Great.

The gator and I stare at each other while I eat my chicken tenders and fries.

CHAPTER TEN

Halloween

The rising sun wakes me. Turns out there are quite a few downsides to sleeping in a car. It's not comfortable, there's nothing to block out the light of day, and I'm still covered in my dinner. Okay, maybe that last one is a plus. I pick a french fry off my chest and eat it.

From the safety of my car I don't see any creatures around that could eat me. Unless those songbirds in the tree are calling their friends to come overwhelm me and peck my eyes out. Shit. One of the birds is now staring at me.

"Don't look at me like that!" I yell, "I have no beef with you, so leave me alone."

The flock erupts out of the tree. Whoa, that's a lot

of birds—a whole lot more than I thought was over there. I shiver as they fly up into the sky and out of sight. Good riddance.

After retrieving my other flip flop from the middle of the yard, which is all muddy now, I try to pick up my case of wine. The cardboard is ruined from the rain and it tears with only a gentle tug. There's a business card in here. One word stands out: Deanna. I toss it into the yard then carry the bottles up onto the porch.

On the left side there's two rocking chairs with a table in the middle, and to the right there's no furniture. It's fine, I probably won't be out here much since it's not screened in.

Moving on, I take one step inside and stop. Luis painted all right. The walls are the brightest freaking shade of yellow I've ever seen. Did I somehow mention a desire to live on the face of the sun? I should have bought sunglasses.

Straight ahead is the living room he furnished with a beige rug that almost covers all the wood flooring, a futon for a couch, wicker coffee table and end tables with one matching chair, a blue entertainment center with one of those huge old televisions, a tall fake palm tree in the corner and some flowery pictures on the walls. It's…well, I don't love it, but I don't hate it either.

The door to the bedroom is on my right. I'll check it after I put this wine in the kitchen. To the left of the front door is the dining room with an ugly brass chandelier hanging down over an oval wood dining table with six—no, seven chairs? Huh. Okay, whatever. There's three windows looking out onto the porch, and two windows on the side wall, which gives a great view of the marsh. Overall, not a bad sitting place.

The kitchen is to the right of the dining room. I set the bottles on the counter. Luis got me appliances: an oven with coil burners on the stovetop which I don't plan on using, a microwave I will use, and he did indeed buy and stock a refrigerator for me. So, of course I could have avoided last night's run-in with the gator.

Ooh, coffee! That sounds good. How do I work this thing? There's only three buttons on the front, but I forget the ratio of coffee to water.

Up north I had the fancy pre-packaged coffee that made one cup at a time. I remember pestering Dave for a whole year to agree to get one. His argument was he usually woke up first, which meant he made coffee more often than me, therefore he should get to keep his Star Wars themed coffee maker. Little did he know, it wasn't the appliance that bothered me, it was that he made terrible coffee.

One day, the coffee was especially bad and I finally yelled at him about it. In hindsight, I know he was just being defensive because I was so mad, but he actually yelled back at me to make my own damn coffee. So I bought my machine and set it up next to his. This was probably the most ridiculous argument of our entire marriage, and it lasted a week until he tried a cup of my coffee. I think if I had handled things differently, we could have had another week of happiness.

The coffee is done brewing now. I rummage through the cabinets and find Luis stocked them with plates and bowls, pots and pans, silverware, tupperware, glasses and mugs. The mugs are all different sizes with various inspirational sayings or cheery pictures. Obviously he hand picked them. I'm tempted to shatter some of them into a million pieces for their stupidity, but then one catches my eye that simply says, "Relax & Enjoy."

I sip my coffee, which tastes awful by the way, as I shuffle through the living room and into my bedroom. Ugh. It's yellow too. Oh well. Nice plush mattress, just like he said. Lavender sheets and flowery coverlet, with a pretty wire headboard and footboard, three pictures of flying birds above the bed, oak night tables on either side with simple little lamps, and a dresser with a clunky old television. One window with —Ooh! blackout curtains. Perfect. I shut them. Thankfully, it tones down the yellow.

There's another fake palm tree in the corner. I'm going to have to move that. It looks like a creepy shadow person. I grab it and drag it out onto the front porch.

As soon as I step outside, one of those flying roaches crawls out from the tree onto my arm. Shit! I drop the tree, flail my arms, then pat myself down from head to toe. It's scurrying around in the tree somewhere now. I can hear it. I shiver and grab the top leaves and drag it, running down the steps and around to the right side of the house where the forest is and leave it.

Then I check the porch to make sure it didn't jump off mid-journey. No sign of it. That better be the last bug I encounter. They creep me out more than birds.

I gaze around my surroundings, letting the breeze waft under my tank top. Overall, Luis did a good job with what I gave him to work with. Hell, I would be curled up on the floor of this place otherwise. I lucked out meeting him. Bet Brenda would like him too. Oh, hell, stop thinking! I don't want to think about anything, least of all her.

There's a car coming down my driveway. Why? Why? Why? I plant my fists on my hips. It's not Luis, I know he has a white mini-van now.

It's freaking Deanna.

She gets out of the car and hollers, "What's up, lady? What's happenin'? Nice digs!"

"Go away."

"You look like you had a rough night. Should've called me." She steps up onto my porch.

She's got some nerve. I go inside but she was apparently following me so closely that she's in my living room before I could turn to shut the door in her face like I planned.

"I brought brunch." She holds up a clear bag with to-go boxes inside.

Well, no point in wasting free food. I take a box and sit on the futon to eat. This isn't brunch, this is a muffin and a cheese danish. Whatever.

She starts yammering on like Brenda used to do. I don't even care how she found out where I live. Shit, she probably followed me home! I eye her up and down while she's walking around and eating, probably dropping crumbs all over the place.

There! A chunk of her muffin fell on the floor and I bet she's not even going to pick it up. And now she stepped on it. Great.

"Okay. Time to go. I'm very busy." I usher her toward the door.

When I open it, Luis is standing there with his fist in the air like he was about to knock.

"Oh, hi May. I wanted to check in on you to see how you like everything."

I pinch my nose between my eyes. "Yep. It's all great."

He walks inside because I guess he thought I was

holding the door open for him.

Deanna shakes his hand, "Hi, I'm Deanna."

"I'm Luis, the realtor. How do you know May?"

"Oh, we go way back."

I jump, "No. We don't. I met her last night at a bar and she just showed up here."

He eyes Deanna, then looks at me... differently. I can't put my finger on—Oh no.

"It's not what you think."

He holds his hands up as if to portray his lack of judgment on the matter.

I sit on the futon to finish my 'brunch'. They continue talking. I'm pretending every time her mouth opens she sounds like monkey hooting and hollering, and when he talks he makes a goat sound. Then I change it around and make her a goat and him an elephant. Wait... she opens her mouth, throwing her head back in laughter —there's the elephant. Yes.

He says, "You should come, May."

Damn, I should have been listening. Come on, think of an excuse... "Can't. Uh, car won't start." That should be good enough.

"Oh, no! Want me to call the dealership and have them fix it? There should be nothing wrong with it so soon like this."

"It's my fault. There was a gator so I slept in my car."

"Should've called me," says Deanna, holding out her necklace, "This is an alligator tooth. I don't hunt them or anything, but I do catch them. I wear this as a reminder of the danger involved and the respect they deserve."

Gross. What kind of person wears a tooth around

their neck?

Luis puts his hand on my shoulder, "Glad you're okay… It's probably the battery, let me take a look."

She says, "I'm parked closer. I'll jump it."

I sit at the dining table. If I lock the door now, would they go away? Or would they knock until I answered? Let's see. I lock the door, lean against it and wait.

A few minutes later the doorknob rattles. Now one of them is indeed knocking. No luck for me today.

When I open the door, they're both standing there, and Luis has a red gun. I gasp, stumble backwards, lose my footing and fall to the ground.

He says, "I'm so sorry! It's only a flare gun, I promise."

"You scared the crap out of me!" I yell.

Deanna's giggling as she offers me her hand to help me up.

I stand up on my own.

Luis says, "I wanted to give this to you. You should have one since your house is so secluded and so close to the marsh. I'm sure that's not the last gator you're going to see."

Great. Just freaking great.

He continues, "I'll put it over here on the end table next to your Limpkin book. By the way, did you like it? Very informative, no? I read it while working on your place."

I nod, but, really? I didn't even know the book was there.

Deanna says, "So, you guys want to go to Pinky's later?"

He says, "That sounds like fun, but I'm taking my

kids around the neighborhood."

She turns to me, "What do you think?" Then she sings, "There's going to be a costume contest!"

"No."

She continues, "Oh, c'mon. They don't decorate or anything until today, partly because they get too many weirdos—I learned that word from you. So they do all the decorating today and have one party, this one night only, so big it spills out into the parking lot where I hear they're setting up a haunted house!"

"Why would they do that on some random night? Sounds stupid to me."

"Well, Halloween. Duh."

Oh no. A wave of nausea crashes into me. I need air. Can't breathe. My heart is racing, my vision is blurry. I push past them, out onto the porch, and sit on the steps, burying my head in my hands.

Almost in unison, they say, "You okay?" and sit on either side of me. One of them is rubbing my back.

"What is it?" asks Luis, "Did something happen around Halloween? Something to do with your family?"

"My daughter's birthday."

Deanna says, "I didn't know you had kids. Well, shoot, we can skip Pinky's and go trick-or-treating with her if you want. Maybe go with his kids around his neighborhood."

I glare at her.

Luis says, "It's okay, I understand. We'll leave you in peace, but if you decide you want to be around people instead, I'm here for you."

Peace? Ugh.

He leads her away. The sickness is less but still lingering, and it's too bright out here. I need to get to my bedroom, to the picture of my baby girl, to the letter she wrote me, the last thing I have that she touched and created.

As I'm crawling my way back inside the house I hear Luis say to her, "She's grieving."

CHAPTER ELEVEN

Merry Christmas?

My old routine is wrapped around me again like a soft blanket. The days and nights are cooler now, I think. I haven't really been outside. Sometimes I catch myself wondering how much time has gone by, but then I stop. I don't care.

What I do care about is food, and I'm out of what Luis had stocked for me. I kind of wish Brenda was here to do the shopping. Kind of. Guess I'm taking a trip into town.

I get dressed in my shorts and tank top, then find my car keys and wallet, and slip on my flip flops. When I step outside it's too chilly to wear this, so I go back in and change into the purple track suit and put on my old sneakers.

Heading to the car, the day is about half over, judging by the sun in the clear blue sky. I better make this quick so I don't get stuck driving at night. I'd put it off until tomorrow but I literally have nothing left to eat in the house.

I stop at my mailbox at the end of my dirt driveway. Ugh, I forgot about mail. I pull up, reach out the window, grab the small stack and I lose my grip on them all and they fall into my lap. I gather them up then sift through them. Bills, bills and more bills, plus some colored envelopes. Oh, and my official license plate for my car. I'll have to stop somewhere to put it on. Being responsible sucks.

I set the bills aside then inspect the first colored envelope, which is brown. Shit, it's from Brenda. She freaking found me! Inside is a letter:

Dearest sister,

I'm thinking of you always, but especially now at Thanksgiving. I know you're having a hard time dealing with your emotions, so I'm giving you your space. Just know I love you and I'm thankful for you. I'm here when you need me. I hope someday we can be close again like we used to be.

I Love You,
Brenda

Yeah, well, if she weren't so smothering and annoying and always trying to spend the settlement money, then maybe we could be close again. I toss the letter out the window. Here's another envelope with her name on it that has a Christmas tree stamp. Christmas? Ugh, I'm not even going to open it. I toss it out the window too.

What could this yellow envelope be? Seriously? This one's from Deanna, but she's inviting herself to come to my house and eat with me for Thanksgiving. She must be crazy. That's not how invitations work.

Ah-ha! This one is from her too. I figured as much. Yep, it's a Christmas card. Why do they bother?

Huh, a little orange envelope with no name and I don't recognize the return address. I open it. It's an invitation to Thanksgiving dinner from Luis, Isabella, Sofia and Zoe. Nope, not going to happen. Wait, if Brenda and Deanna sent a Christmas card, then Thanksgiving has passed already anyway. Ha! Oh well! Got out of that one. No Christmas card from Luis though?

I find my map in the car, stare at it, then head to town. The route is so simple I can't believe I even needed the map. Turn left from my driveway and that turns into the main road in town.

Once the trees turn to buildings on either side of the road I know I'm officially in Rise, and I notice all the light posts have giant candy canes and Christmas trees made out of tinsel or something attached to them.

There's a check-cashing business on the right, and one of the advertisements on the window says, 'Pay your bills here!' so I pull in.

Inside, there's a white, fake Christmas tree all decorated and lit up. Ridiculous. Christmas trees should only be green, with maybe a hint of white to look like snow. White is as bad as those pink or purple ones the stores started selling years ago.

I lay out my mail on the nearest little counter, in front of a young woman behind glass who greets me, with extra friendly holiday-spirit, "How can I help you?"

"Paying some bills."

"Okay, I'd be happy to help you with that."

I start opening the envelopes.

"How much would you like to pay?"

"Well, I have to pay what the bill says, right?" I sound a little condescending, but I actually want to know.

"Some people pay ahead, some people can only afford half. It's up to you." She picks up a couple bills, "But these are a little overdue, so you should pay the full amount to avoid incurring extra late fees."

"I'll pay extra."

"Okie-dokie."

I'm tapping my finger on the counter. She finishes shuffling through my bills then smiles at me. Neither of us speak. Is she waiting for me? Fine. "And, how do I do that?"

"Oh, you need to sign up for an account with us, then as long as you have a check and your ID, then you're good to go."

Great, I have one check left in my wallet. The woman helps me through the process and I pay enough extra on each bill to last several months.

I turn to leave and the lady says, "Have a great day, and Merry Christmas!"

"Yeah, right." I mumble, then hurry out.

Now I also need to stop at the bank to order more checks, if it's still open. I should have asked where it is instead of driving around, but I couldn't stand to be near her cheerful attitude any longer.

Down the road there's a bank on each corner of

the intersection. One of them is the same bank I used up north which is a bit of good luck but, of course, I have to pass the intersection, merge to the left lane, do a u-turn, then make a hard right to pull in. Naturally, my gas light comes on. Whatever, might as well add yet another stop to make.

There's only minutes to spare before they close, so I rush over to a teller. Ordering my checks is easy, except for remembering my address beyond 44 Limpkin.

"Look it up on your phone," says the bank teller who looks like he should still be in high school.

"I don't have a—."

He pulls his fancy smartphone out of his pocket and seconds later he's filling in my city, state and zip code for me.

"Anything else I can help you with?"

"Yeah." I was going to withdraw some cash, but I think I already did that, and didn't spend any. Where did I put it? Eh, I'll find it. "Never mind. Got a stairway to Heaven hidden in the back somewhere?"

He laughs, so I walk away.

In my car I check the glove compartment and find my cash, right where I must have left it. I put it in my wallet then drive out of the bank parking lot.

As soon as I reach the middle of the road to make a left, I see a gas station on the right. The road looks clear, so I crank the wheel to the right. A horn blares at me then a little car comes out of nowhere and swerves around me. Shit!

I run over a curb, lose my grip on the steering wheel for a moment, almost hit a stupid pigeon, then come to a stop just inside the gas station parking lot. Ugh. Come on, May.

Pulling up to a pump, I'm taking a chance my tank is on the driver's side. For once, I'm right! Before I can get out, an older man comes toward me with a piece of paper in his hand. He's smiling and appears overall non-threatening with his casual, limping way of walking.

At my window, he says, with only a slight southern accent, "Sorry for the inconvenience, ma'am, but this pump's outta order." He tapes the paper on the pump. "You'll have to move over to another one."

I'm not surprised. This usually happens to me. Sometimes it was so bad that even when I would be in the car with Dave, he would be somehow steered by my bad-luck day, as he called it, to the only pump not working, or the one parking spot with broken glass littered in it, because apparently that never happened to him alone. I guess this is the beginning of one of those days, but I was doing so good until now.

At a working pump, the man is still loitering around picking up a couple stray pieces of trash. Maybe that's a stroke of good luck? I get out and ask, "I'm going to get some gas, but do you have the tools to put on my license plate for me?"

"Well, sure! That's a simple fix. Let's go inside and get your gas set up, then I'll put it on for ya while you pump. You get that beauty in town?"

"Yeah."

"Then you got a good deal. Nice folks that family… So, I haven't seen you around before, you stayin' or passin' through?"

"Staying."

"Then you'll be happy to know this is a safe little town. We look out for one another 'round here."

I nod.

"How much gas you want?"

"Well, the light came on, how much do you think it'll take?"

"Twenty-five ought to do it."

"Okay."

I pump my gas while he puts on my license plate and yammers on more about the town. The sun is slowly falling in the sky and I feel the pressure of getting back to the house before dark.

He says, "So, if you ever need any help, come by or give us a call."

"Where's the grocery store?"

"Go that way toward the main road and make a left and you'll see it on the right after a couple blocks."

"Thanks." I get in my car.

"Merry Christmas!"

I wave and drive away.

The grocery store is right where he said it would be, and turns out it's across the street from Pinky's, which is bursting with people. Deanna's probably there too, she better not see me. I shield my face with my hands as I run inside.

Of course, if anyone were to be looking for a graying, middle-aged woman in a purple track suit, they could spot me easily. At least she doesn't know what I'm wearing— I hope.

What the—It looks like Christmas threw up all over the place in here. I grab a cart and head straight to the canned goods aisle where I load up on tuna, chicken, baked beans, green beans, various fruits, raviolis, soups, ramen noodles, anything that'll keep the longest. When the cart is almost full I stop.

A quick stop in the coffee aisle, I grab a few

containers of different flavors of ground coffee. Eh, I better get a few more. I've become used to coffee each morning again, just like when Dave was alive.

Next I make my way over to the paper products and shove as many packages of toilet paper that will fit on the shelf underneath the cart. Then I hit the wine aisle. Why don't they have the Fancy Feathers brand I got from Pinky's? Oh well. I pick the cheapest merlot and gently stack about twenty bottles on top of the canned goods in my cart. Just freaking great, now I can hardly push this thing!

I'm out of breath now I've trudged around the corner to a checkout line. Ooh, candy bars. I grab a bunch and put them right onto the short conveyor belt that moves them closer to the cashier to ring up. I have to unload everything else onto the belt too.

I ask the cashier, "Can I get help with—" Then the light bouncing off her hair catches my eye and I find myself mesmerized. She has the most beautiful, voluminous afro I've ever seen. Annie loved the hairstyle too, she called it happy-hair.

"Ma'am?"

"Sorry… your hair is so pretty."

"Oh, thanks! I appreciate that, I do it myself."

I smile and nod while running my fingers through my thin, stringy hair, pondering whether it could be happy like that. Probably not.

Next thing I know, there's two teenage boys unloading, bagging and re-loading all my groceries for me. My total comes to just under four hundred dollars. This stuff better last me months! The cashier wishes me a Merry Christmas and I don't even think to say it back because I'm taking in a last look at her hair.

One of the boys helps me pack my car. I'm so grateful I dig in my wallet, pull out a five dollar bill and hold it out to him. I might even wish him a Merry Christmas.

He says, "No, thank you."

What? "Take it." When has a kid his age ever refused money? Is my tip not good enough?

"It's just policy. Merry Christmas." And he walks away, taking my empty cart too.

I'm standing here, still holding the five dollar bill, staring at him. Oh well.

My car is running a little slow, but the sun is only starting to set, so I roll down my window and let the crisp breeze caress my cheeks.

Overall it's actually been a good day, a little strange, but good. I smile to myself. I'll even make it home before dark.

Wait. Home!? I scowl and grip the steering wheel tight. How could I possibly call that shack my home? What an insult to my family in heaven! It's just a house. What is wrong with me?

And to top it off, I made it through all my errands without running in to any prying questions! No freaking Brenda, Luis, or Deanna. Nobody cares. It's Christmas and no one has come to check on me! I hate them all.

I don't care if anyone checks on me or not. I don't care about anything and that's fine until one day, hopefully soon, I'll die and get to be with my family again. I'm not here to live, I'm biding my time. Everyone else can go to hell! I scream, "Go to hell!"

Back at the stupid house, I grab two stupid grocery bags, which is all I can carry because they're so heavy, and stomp my way up onto the porch. I'm not in the mood for any wildlife bullshit tonight, so I leave the bags there and go back for another two.

Several trips to the car later, I have all the bags safely by the front door. Seriously? Not even an alligator cares to attack me anymore? I guess it's what I've wanted, and now I'm getting it. So, that's just freaking fine! I don't care. Ugh, now I have to get all the bags into the house.

As I pick up the last bag, I notice a little package wrapped in Christmas paper. Where did this come from? It must have been someone else's at the grocery store and I grabbed it by mistake.

Instead of putting the groceries away, I'm sitting at the dining table, staring at the little package, because, what's the rush? It's all non-perishable stuff.

What if this present *is* meant for me? Pfft, probably not, no one would think to do something like that for me. I didn't exactly give out any gifts either. But at the same time, I'm not going to drive back into town to return it, so I deem it mine.

I tear off the wrapping paper which reveals a plain brown box. Huh, it's not small enough to be jewelry, but it's not big enough to be anything other than a rock. Guess I'm saving someone from an awkward, 'thank you' for a terrible gift.

Inside a wad of green tissue paper is a little felt bag, but there's something else in the bottom of the box. Yep, it's actually a freaking rock. I turn it over. The word 'Peace' is carved into it and painted gold. Okay, that's better, at least it's a rock with a purpose.

Time to see what's in the felt bag. I stick my fingers in it to widen the opening then tip it over onto the counter. A necklace falls out. Aw. A gold chain with an angel pendant. The angel's dress is a chunk of cut crystal and the wings and head are gold. Probably plated, but it's cute. I kind of like it.

Now I feel bad. This is probably someone's gift to their granddaughter. But I have no way of returning it because even if I get it back to the grocery store, how are they going to find who it belongs to? There's no name or anything. Wait, a mini Christmas card with a picture of a tiny winter landscape on the front. Inside it reads:

Dear May,

Wishing you peace and comfort during this Christmas season. Know your loved ones are still with you in spirit.

Your friend,
Luis

My eyes well up. I take it all back. I don't want Luis or anyone to go to hell. I'm sorry! God, I'm so sorry.

For hours I read the card and look at the rock and necklace, contemplating my life. Why am I alone? What is the point of any of this? I have no purpose anymore—my purpose is dead. Are these things supposed to be a sign that I'll be with my family soon? Or that I won't?

I hang the necklace on the latch of the dining room window so it will hopefully reflect rainbows in the daylight. Annie loved rainbows. Then I bring the rock into the bedroom where I place it next to my family picture.

CHAPTER TWELVE

The Bird

Well, I'm awake for yet another day. When will the monotony end? Day after day after day I have to endure my broken heart alone, eat alone, sleep alone… The only thing I wouldn't mind doing alone is dying because I would be greeted by my family. Some day…

The phone rings. Huh, so that thing does work. It rings again. Well, I guess there's no harm in seeing who it is. "Hello?"

"May? It's Brenda!"

Shit. I hang up.

A few minutes pass, then it rings again. I knew it! I knew she'd call back. I'm not going to answer it. Finally it stops while I make a bowl of ramen noodles for breakfast.

I kind of thought she'd call back one more time, but apparently not. Good. I sit at the dining table and in between spoonfuls of soup I stare at the angel necklace still hanging in the window. Stupid thing hasn't even made rainbows.

Lying on the futon in the living room, I can't decide if I want to turn the TV on or not. It's always a toss-up whether the show or commercial will be some smiling happy family, or something I can tolerate. Eh, let's see.

It's a commercial: A young couple sitting at a romantic dinner. The guy sets a small box on the table and slides it over to her. The woman opens it—it's a diamond necklace—and she cries. Then the narrator says, "This Valentines day, get her a gift she'll really love."

Gross. She's probably crying because that necklace is hideous. It's pretty hard to screw up diamonds, but this company has apparently been successful at it. I turn the TV off.

Dave was the best at Valentines gifts. His were simple and touching. One year he surprised me with tickets to this acrobatic show I had been dying to see, where they all dress up in these crazy costumes. There was singing and dancing and even flying. We didn't have great seats, but for a show like that it was better to be farther away to take in all that was going on.

The only thing I didn't like about his gifts was they made mine seem so terrible. I wasn't creative like he was. That same year I had gotten him a tie. He said he loved it, but I knew it was bad—it had little lights in it and if you pressed a button hidden in the flap it would play some romantic tunes. Every year I would tell myself I'm going to do better and every year I tried, but ultimately failed by comparison.

Annie got her creativity from him, or my parents, or both. She would always hand-make a card in the shape of a heart for Dave and I both. They're probably all still in a shoebox somewhere in my house up north, if Brenda didn't get rid of them. She better not be touching any of my stuff. I'd go up there to get some things if I knew she wasn't going to be there.

I make myself a cup of coffee. Maybe I'll go outside today…and maybe it'll be snowing! Wouldn't that be something? Snow in Florida. I wonder how cold it is up north? Brenda's probably shoveling my driveway right now. Ha!

What is that? Is someone knocking at the door? Someone came to visit! Ugh, now I have to get up.

Well, there's no one outside my door and it's pretty cold actually, though not cold enough to snow. No little gift or anything either. Maybe I should walk down to my mailbox to see if my bills need to be paid again. Nah, my lights are still working so I'm still good.

Where the hell is the knocking coming from? Now it sounds more like tapping. I check the kitchen, but the faucet isn't dripping. What could it be?

Now the sound is coming from behind me. At the dining room window where the necklace is hanging, there's this bird on my porch about two feet tall with long legs and a long curved beak, pecking at the glass. It's probably trying to eat my little angel. Stupid bird.

Where else can I put it? I don't want to wear it because I have a hard enough time remembering to change my clothes. I put it in the bedroom next to the Peace rock, where it should have been all along since it won't even reflect rainbows like I wanted it to.

When I come out of the bedroom, the bird is still pecking at the window. I sit at the dining table. "Hey, stupid! What do you want?"

It stops and cocks its head.

"What do you want?"

Now it's pecking again. How long will it keep going until it realizes the necklace isn't there any more? I wait as long as I can and the bird is still tapping on the window. This is ridiculous.

I march out and yell, "Shoo! Shoo! Shoo!" while waving my arms.

It doesn't even flinch.

"Go away! Shoo!" I stomp my feet.

Then it lets out a high-pitched wail, "Krrr-eeeow!"

What the hell? I try to imitate it, but I can't get my voice that high.

It screams again, "Krrr-eeeow! Keow! Keow!"

How dare this bird come up onto my porch and scream at me! I flap my arms wildly and jump around, "Shoooooooo!"

"Krrr."

It's still not leaving. "Fine, stay here for now, but you better be gone when I come out again."

It can't loiter here forever. I shut myself in the bedroom and lay down. What a rude bird. Damn it, I can still hear it from here. Reminds me of Brenda and her constant nagging. I imagine the bird with her face and each tap is a word out of her mouth saying, "May,-you-should-change-your-clothes," or, "May,-let's-go-shop-ping". Now I picture her as if she's shaped like the bird, with skinny legs, wings instead of arms, and lips that droop and hang like the bird's long beak. Ha! Now there's a sight.

Maybe it's one of those Limpkins? I search for the book in the living room that I'm pretty sure Luis was telling me about. I find it. Good, I wasn't imagining that, the book is real and it's here with the flare gun. I guess my brain doesn't think about stuff until it matters.

I sit at the dining table and flip through it. Looks like the same type of bird: Long dark legs, brown body with white spots, long neck speckled with lots of white, the beak is long and curved downward, and it stands just over two feet tall. Yep, must be a Limpkin.

This says they mostly eat apple snails, so why does it want the window? The bird stops pecking and we stare at each other.

I continue reading. They're not aggressive, but the males are territorial with other birds. That's good. Some fear humans and some don't, depending on their interaction. This one is obviously not afraid of me. I'm kind of creeped out it won't stop staring at me, cocking it's head side to side like it's trying to figure out if I'll fit down it's throat. Gross.

Well, I'm going to go about my day and ignore it… Ugh, I can feel it's eyes on me in the kitchen, and in the living room too. I peek over my shoulder, and sure enough it's there, staring at me.

I turn on the TV in the bedroom to the shopping channel and lay in bed.

A while later, I'm hungry again. The monotony of eating is disturbing. How great would it be if we as humans didn't have to eat unless we *wanted* to, to taste something different? That would be nice. I bet my family doesn't have to eat in Heaven. I picture them with angel wings, playing in fluffy white clouds and rainbows. Damn it, I want to be with them.

I drag myself out to the kitchen. Out of the corner of my eye I can see the bird is still there, and I'm not sure if it ever left. It's eating a snail the size of an apple. That must be where they got the name. Gross.

What do *I* want to eat? Nothing looks appetizing. Ramen noodles it is. I sit at the dining table to eat, next to the window where the bird is right on the other side.

Maybe I should name it, since it's apparently not going anywhere. I flip through the Limpkin book. Males and females are hard to distinguish, except males are more vocal. Well, then I deem this one a male by the way it screamed at me before.

I tap on the glass. "What's your name, bird?"

He looks at me.

"Your name, dummy."

Now he's distracted, but I can't tell with what. Fine, I'll figure something out. Lets see, Limpkin is the type of bird, so I could just call him that. Eh, I find that hard to say. The book says they are also known as Crying Birds. Interesting. Maybe he wasn't screaming earlier, but was actually crying?

Maybe I'll call him C.B.? Nah. I tap my fork into my now empty bowl and the bird mimics me by pecking on the window. Kind of annoying, but cute too. Annie used to mimic me when she was little. While I was doing the dishes she would move her hands around by my side like she was washing invisible dishes.

I don't need these reminders. Hopefully the bird goes away, then I won't name it and it won't remind me of my daughter. I put my bowl in the sink then retreat back to the bedroom where I'm out of the bird's watchful eye.

∞ • ∞

Every time I wake up, it's a different time of day or night, which makes it hard to keep track of time—not that I'm trying to. Okay, now it's daylight, but I'm not sure how many days have passed. A couple? Several? More than several? Either way, I'm still tired. I'm always kind of tired. I roll to my right, then my left, and now I have to go to the bathroom. Another annoying thing humans have to do. It's all we really do, well it's all I do now anyway. What goes in must come out. So monotonous.

Now I'm laying on the living room floor, trying not to think about the bird that's *still* outside the window. It's as unsettling as having a person waiting around for me. I swear the TV in the bedroom just said Saint Patrick's Day, so it's been like a month? Hm. As I'm thinking, I notice the room is turning kind of orange. I sit up and see out the window that it's very orange outside. Guess it'll be dark soon, again.

The phone rings. I pick it up, but don't say anything.

"Hello? May?… Hello?" then a dial tone.

Ha! It was Brenda. She probably thinks she dialed the wrong number. She'll call back. I wait.

I'm still waiting after an hour. I can't believe she's not calling back! Maybe I'll call her and yell at her. I start to dial her number, but I can't remember it. Oh well. Guess she doesn't care *that* much about me.

"Krrr-eeeow! Keow! Keow! Keow!" The bird screams.

That's it, enough. I get to my feet, march out onto the porch and face it with my hands on my hips. "What do you want? Why are you hanging around?"

The bird cocks his little head.

"No food for you here. Go away."

He doesn't budge. There's no reasoning with this one I guess.

I boldly move closer and yell, "Shoo!"

The bird looks huge as it stands on his toes and stretches his wings out.

"Go away!" I scream.

"Krrr-eeeow! Keow! Keow! Keow!" he screams back at me.

This is ridiculous.

In my pajamas, I storm out into the yard and head for the marsh. My toes sink deeper into the muck as I get closer to the water. What was I thinking? There could be any little bug or critter lurking, waiting for an opportunity to snack on me. I roll my pant legs up a little, real quick, so they don't get muddy, then hurry down to the water's edge.

Better not be any gators... Where are all the freaking snails? Ah-ha! Found some. I grab two from the muck, one in each hand, then run as best as I can, lifting my knees high to get out of the marshy area.

The bird is waiting for me on the porch. Somehow he looks amused. It's probably my imagination since I've never seen their faces show expressions or emotions or anything.

"Here, bird, want this?" I wave one snail around and I catch his attention.

His head is moving around in circles to watch it. Perfect. I've got him right where I want him. When I throw this snail far away, the bird will go after it. Then I'll throw the other one to keep it busy for a while and away from the house.

The snail is slimy and when I try to throw it I lose my grip and it bounces and rolls to a stop at the bird's feet. Great. Really freaking great. "Not my intention, bird!"

"Keow!"

He seems pleased. Now he's jabbing his beak into the opening of the shell. I can't believe he wasn't scared, like he somehow knew I couldn't throw that far. I blame the slime.

Well, I might as well catch my breath while he eats. If I throw the other one now he probably won't notice, so I set the second snail on the floor. I sit down next to it and lean my back against the house right next to the front door, just in case.

Oh, that reminds me. I have a flare gun. Hm… That would scare it for sure, but it's supposed to be my 'just in case' for alligators. A vision pops into my head of me shooting it and accidentally setting the bird on fire… Yeah, I can't do that. I mean, I don't like birds but that doesn't mean I want to burn one alive. Plus, Dave and Annie would be upset with me if I did that, even by accident.

The bird pulls the snail out of its shell in one smooth movement. Gross. Oh no, he's coming toward me. What do I do? He's so tall we are almost at eye level since I'm sitting on the floor. Now he's right in front of me. I close my eyes as tight as I can.

Nothing is happening. I peek. He's…giving it to me?

Slowly shaking my head I utter, "I. Don't. Want."

He dangles it right in front of my face.

"No."

The bird leans in close, aiming the snail toward

my mouth with its long beak. I move my head back as far as it will go without moving my body. Shit, I might *have* to eat this thing!

Then he drops it on my chest.

Seriously? Disgusting.

He takes a step back, but is watching me. "Keow!" he screams.

"Okay! Okay." I pluck it off my chest and struggle to hold it in both hands. This is so freaking gross. What the hell am I doing?

"Keow! Keow!"

I hold the snail up in front of my mouth and pretend to eat it. "Yum." I smile and nod. Then I gag a little, but I don't think he notices.

"Kerr-rr-rr-owh." His call is softer than his scream, more like a cat purring. I get the impression he's pleased with himself and I even see a little smile in his eyes.

Well, I don't want to be rude, but I'm not going to eat this thing either, so I'll try a little magic trick. I keep one hand by my mouth as I hide the snail in my other hand and sneak it down onto the floor next to me, out of his sight. Ha, stupid bird.

Damn it! He found the second snail. Now I'm the stupid one. I should have thrown it already so he would go follow it. He's digging his beak in now. I hope I don't have to pretend to eat this one too.

Oh, thank God. He's eating it himself. Aw, now he's sitting down next to me! I guess all my complaining brought a bird to be my friend. Hm…I don't know how I feel about that.

CHAPTER THIRTEEN

Limpy

The sun does indeed set over my view of the marsh, and boy does it put on a show. The sky is purple and pink with some deep red around the sun. There's a few thin clouds obstructing the sunlight, creating rays of bright yellow, lightly touching the tips of the tall golden-brown grasses swaying in the gentle breeze. I'm surprised this is the first time I'm noticing it.

Limpy is still sitting next to me. I've decided to call him that because the book says they walk with a limp. I hadn't noticed, but it's a cute name and it's easy to say. It's kind of nice to have someone sit with me, though he'll probably leave me eventually like everyone else.

Maybe I'm wrong about birds altogether? Maybe

they're not all cold and calculating and always looking for their next thing to poop on. Annie had such a connection with animals that sometimes I swore she was having full conversations with them. She had even managed to train a couple of the songbirds in the backyard to land on her hand to get the treat she was holding.

"Where are you going?" I ask as he walks away from me and down into the yard.

Oh, he had to poop. That's considerate—for a bird —to walk away and do his business elsewhere. Well, I might as well take this opportunity to get up without him potentially attacking me. I shut myself inside, then watch out the dining window. He's walking back up the steps. Aw, he looks confused. I tap on the glass and he runs over to me.

"Keow! Keow."

"Yeah, but I can't stay out there all night. I'll be right inside here."

"Keow."

I open a can of some kind of pre-made spaghetti in the shape of little letter O's with sauce, heat it up, then sit at the dining table to eat and watch Limpy.

He's pacing back and forth in front of the window and pecking at the glass every few steps. I think he's trying to find a way in. Hope he doesn't, I don't want to have to clean up after him.

"Krrr-eeeow. Keow. Keow." His cries sound less like screaming and more like actual crying.

Poor thing. I feel bad for him, but what am I supposed to do? I tap on the window. "Don't get eaten by anything. I'll see you in the morning."

"Krrr-eeeow!"

I say louder, "Good night."

"Krrr-eeeow! Keow! Keow! Keow!"

Ugh. I open the front door and he stops. "Good bird. Be quiet." I shut the door.

"Keow! Keow!"

I fling the door open. "What the hell is your problem? I'm right inside here! Quit your cryin'!" Hearing myself, I'm reminded of the time when my Annie was only seven years old and her hamster had died. She cried for a week and I couldn't stand it anymore so I told her the same thing, to quit her crying. Now that she's gone, I regret every single time I yelled at her, and especially that time because she was only a child and she was grieving.

"Krrr-eeeow! Keow! Keow! Keow!"

I almost don't want to leave him, but I can't be friends with a bird. Hopefully I can fall asleep quick. I go into the bedroom to read Annie's letter. Limpy is still crying outside. I turn the volume up on the TV, but I can still hear him.

Ugh, I can't get comfortable. I've been listening to him for so long now I don't know if he's even there anymore, or if I'm imagining the sound and playing it over and over in my head. Nah, I'm not that crazy, right?

Actually, that did happen once before, when my daughter was still a baby. She cried for a whole month straight, no matter what I did. Poor Dave had to sleep on the couch downstairs while I stayed in her room and didn't get any sleep at all. I was thankful for Brenda then because she came over and stayed up with her for a few nights so I could sleep. But then, after the crying stopped, I kept hearing it anyway and it took me a week until I got a full night's rest.

My parents called it 'phantom cries'. They had a little name for everything. I miss them. They were in their forties when they had kids, so they passed away peacefully in their seventies, only a month after Annie was born. I think they held on to see my baby girl, who was their only grandchild. Now that I think about it, my daughter helped me find peace with my parents' passing, then Dave's… I'd have been a total wreck if it weren't for Annie. Why can't Brenda be more like her?

I get up to check on my bird. It's pitch dark outside now, but the sound is louder by the dining room window, so I assume it's him. But, what if this is still my imagination? I flick on the porch light. Okay, good, it's really him. Why is he sitting here crying incessantly?

Let's see if there are any answers in the Limpkin book. I blink my eyes a couple times to focus, then flip to the section about their calls. It says the repeated, piercing call is their mating call and—wait, what? I re-read more intently. That's indeed what it says. Huh. I flip to the section about mating. It says the males will extract and feed a snail to the female to begin the bonding process.

So he's crying for me because he thinks I'm his mate? How sad. Maybe he used to have a mate that died, like me. Maybe he had babies that died too. We must be going through the same thing!

I step out onto the porch. He walks over and looks up at me like a child would, like my Annie would, and he's quiet.

"It's okay, buddy. I—I understand now." I kneel down.

"Krrr." He purrs.

"I'll be your friend, but I can't be your mate. Okay?"

"Krrr."

"You're a good friend."

He walks a circle around me, then stops to face me again. We gaze into each other's eyes, and I know we understand each other.

"You miss your family, huh?"

Keow.

"I miss mine too…" My eyes well up.

"Krrr. Koew!"

"I can't stand it either!" I wail as tears gush from my eyes. "I miss them so much!"

"Krrr-eeeow! Krrr-eeeow! Krrr-eeeow!" he cries.

Falling to my hands and knees, I cry "Whyyyy?"

"Krrr."

All my tears pool onto the old wood planks of the porch floor. I ask again, softer now, "Why?"

"Krrr. Krrr," he purrs in such a comforting way part of me can almost feel a consoling hand rubbing my back.

It's not real though. I know I'm alone here with the bird who's standing in front of me, unable to comfort me the way a human would. Pain is still radiating from my heart and soul. I look out at the twinkling stars. "Why, God?"

He doesn't answer, and neither does Limpy. I don't know what I expected, something other than silence I guess. I wipe my face, grab a blanket from inside and sit in the rocking chair on the porch. Limpy snuggles up next to my leg and is sleeping within minutes. I cross my arms to hold the blanket up around my neck, lay my head back and close my eyes, listening to the ambient noise of nocturnal nature.

Ow. My neck. I must have fallen asleep. I can't believe I keep waking up.

The darkness of night is giving way to daylight,

and my bird is nowhere around. His same screams and cries echo from across the marsh. It's much colder now than I thought Florida could ever be. My breath is like a fog machine.

Still wrapped in my blanket, I brew a cup of hot coffee and think about last night, how I should feel better after releasing so much emotion. That's what people say will happen, but I feel about the same, if not worse. Also, where the hell is Limpy? Maybe another alligator came over and ate him instead of me... I can't think about that.

I flip through the Limpkin book to try and find an answer about why he disappeared after starting his supposed bonding process with me, but there's nothing about it. Did I show too much of myself and get abandoned by him too? Am I that unloved even a bird doesn't want to be near me?

CHAPTER FOURTEEN

Rainbow

It's been too many sunsets since I last saw Limpy, and I'm kind of worried now that maybe he got eaten by something and I'll never see him ever again. It's my fault for agreeing to be friends. If I had never spent time with him, he probably wouldn't have stayed around, and maybe he would have moved on to a safer place.

I turn off the TV. The less I'm aware of what day it is the better off I'll be. No reminders of anything. No thinking about things other than what's necessary—like food, though even that sucks now. I'm so sick of eating the same old canned crap, but if I order anything to be delivered, it'll remind me of my family. My life is a no-win situation.

I hear "Keow. Keow. Keow.", but it sounds farther away I think. It's hard to tell because of the pattering of raindrops. Limpy's not on the porch, so I guess that wasn't him. Where could he be? I stand at the dining room window and scan the front yard, which is sunnier than it should be.

Actually, I could use a shower. There's no lightning, so I go outside in my pajamas and stand in the gentle, consistent rain, feeling the muddy earth with my toes. If I was a bird, where would I be? Well, I'd be able to fly, so maybe he's in the oak tree.

Nope. There are a few smaller birds hunkered down, but no Limpkins. "Hey, you guys know where Limpy is?…No? All right." Useless.

I walk over to the marsh, keeping my eyes on my next steps to make sure there's nothing sharp or alive in my way. Damn it, one step too far. My foot sinks up to my ankle and I have to yank it out. I thought there was more solid ground before the marsh. It's probably because it's raining.

When I look up, I'm confronted by a huge rainbow beginning from the far left, arching over the whole expanse of the marsh and ending in the forest canopy on the far right. I've never seen one so close and so full. Each color is as clear as if it were painted on an invisible canvas in the sky.

It's. So. Beautiful. I run and grab a rocking chair and drag it back to the exact spot I was standing. Then I sit down real quick so I can resume staring at the magnificent sight.

Where did it go? What the hell! I was gone for one minute! It's just as well. The clouds are clearing and it's getting warm and muggy, which is undoing my rain shower and my chair is sinking.

As I put the rocking chair back on the porch I wonder, was the rainbow a sign? I had stopped looking for them, but this was practically in my face. If it was a sign, what would it mean? A friendly hello or perhaps it was foretelling of better or worse times to come? Who am I kidding? It was simply a byproduct of nature.

I go inside and strip off my now muddy and sweaty clothes, then take a real shower. I only have a sliver of my bar of soap left, but it's enough for now.

Sitting on the floor, rubbing my hairy legs that remind me of Dave, and eyeing the dusty corners of the room, I wonder some more about the rainbow. It was so amazing, it has to mean something, right?

Maybe, if there is a stairway somewhere on earth that leads up to Heaven, then our loved ones get a rainbow slide to come down and visit? Maybe my Annie slid down into the forest and is making her way to the house right now! My heart almost skips a beat thinking that at any moment the door will open and there will be my beautiful baby girl.

Staying as quiet as possible, I wait.

Is that footsteps on the porch? I jump up and fling open the door. Ugh, it's Limpy— Oh! It's Limpy!

"Where have you been? I missed you!"

"Keow!"

"Who's a good bird?"

"Keow! Keow!"

"Well, I'm glad to see you're okay."

"Krrr-eeeow!"

"Oh, you brought me a snail?"

He digs the snail out from its shell, then swallows it.

111

"I see…that's fine, saves me from going to get you one, silly bird." And I don't have to pretend to eat one either.

"Krrr."

"Want to sit with me for a while?" I move toward the clean rocking chair. Not that I want to sit outside since it's so muggy, but if he wants to then I can always shower again later. It won't be too long now until yet another sunset.

He starts coming toward me, then turns around to face the steps.

"Hey, come here. What do you want? Want to come inside?" I open the front door all the way then stand just inside. "Come on, silly bird. Come on."

"Keow. Keow. Keow." He walks down into the yard.

"Limpy! Get back here right now. You can't disappear again—You just came back!"

He keeps going, toward the marsh.

I follow him. Half of me wants to strangle him and half of me wants to cry. Did he only stop by to let me know he's not dead? Is this a goodbye?

At the edge of the marsh he plucks a snail from the muck.

"Is that one for me?"

Now he's eating it.

"What is your problem? I thought we bonded."

"Krrr-eeeow! Keow! Keow! Keow!"

"Sheesh, okay, so maybe I've been a little selfish." I find a snail and hold it out to him, "Here."

He walks away from me, into the marsh until he's knee-deep, then turns sideways and takes slow steps to search for snails.

"I already got you one." I toss it toward him.

It plops into the murky water right next to him. He jumps and flies a few feet, then resumes his searching without even looking at me.

"I'm sorry. Please come sit with me…on the porch where it's not so hot. I'll get you lots of snails."

"Keow!"

"Yeah? Sound good?" I search around and only find one, then look up at Limpy, "I got your— Watch out!" I charge into the marsh, kicking water at him with each step. "Alligator! Alligator, damn it—fly away!" Finally I'm close enough my frantic splashing soaks him and he flies up, narrowly escaping the lunging jaws of the reptile, soars over my head and lands by the house.

My heart is racing, but I'm okay, and he's okay. Everything is okay. Shit! The gator! I scramble out of the marsh and up onto dry land.

I march up to the stupid bird, pointing my finger at him, "You have to pay attention! Actually, you're not allowed to go into the marsh anymore. Next time you're hungry, you tell me and I'll get you your snails, got it?"

He flies away, straight over the middle of the marsh. "Limpy!" Gah! This bird is going to be the death of me. I glare at him in the red-orange sky until he's only a dot, then I lose him in all the other dots flying around in the distance.

I have to take another freaking shower. Two in one day, Brenda would be so proud. I scrub and rinse as fast as I can, then park myself in the rocking chair on the porch. He has to come back eventually, right? So I'll just sit here until he does.

Days later and I've decided he must be one of the dots flying around on the far side of the marsh. Some nerve he has, staying in sight but never coming over to see me. Maybe I need to sit out here earlier, or later in the day? Eh, it's worth a shot, it's not like I'm busy with anything else.

Night after night, still no sign of my bird. I think I'm stressed out about it too, I keep eating to pass the time. If only Annie was here with me...of course, if she were, I wouldn't even be in Florida and I would never have met Limpy. I wonder if she sent him to me? She did always have a way with birds.

More and more days pass. I can't believe he won't come back! This is ridiculous. Is this really what I've become? Some crazy lady who waits for a bird? I'm the human, I'm smarter than he is, I should be able to make him come!

Under the shade of my oak tree, on a pleasantly warm day, I cup my hands on the sides of my mouth and yell as loud as I can so my voice will travel across the marsh, "Limpy!"

All the songbirds evacuate the area. I wait. How can I protect him if he won't even come when called? I bite my fingernail and it hurts, so I inspect my fingers. I've chewed off all my nails just like when Annie was going to camp. Is this a sign? Is Limpy going to die next?

I need something to eat to take my mind off everything. Rummaging through the cupboards and the fridge is fruitless. There's nothing to eat. How could this be? I freaking stocked up! Where's Brenda when I need her? Oh, right, she's living in my house up north, probably dating and fornicating all over my stuff. "Stop thinking!" I yell at myself.

Maybe I'll starve to death... My body will rot and nobody will find me for months and I won't care because

I'll be with my family! Then I get a vivid picture in my mind of myself all rotted and decayed and I shiver. No, I can't die that way. I want it to be simple, like one day I don't wake up, but someone finds me before I rot.

I sit on the porch and chew my hair. Then, a while later, my stomach grumbles so loud I can hear it. I drink a glass of water and lay down in bed. If I could just fall asleep then I can deal with food tomorrow.

CHAPTER FIFTEEN

Surprise!

Well, it's late morning now and I've had four cups of coffee to keep my stomach from yelling at me. It's kind of working, but now I can't help chewing my nails, and the skin around my nails. Gross.

"Get your shit together, May. This is ridiculous!" I say to myself assertively.

Then I answer in a softer tone, "I know, I know. I'm pathetic."

"You're not pathetic, you're hungry. Go into town, buy some food, come straight back. Easy."

"But I don't want to. All those people…"

"Just get your ass dressed."

"But all my clothes are dirty."

"That's never stopped you before! Shorts and a tank top, lets go."

"Fine." I get dressed.

Then, as I'm walking toward the car, I take a minute to look around for Limpy. Maybe he's never coming back. I don't want to think about that.

My assertive self speaks again, "Quit dawdling! Food!"

Right, right. I hurry and get in the car. Hallelujah! There's a candy bar! It's melted and deformed, but I devour it anyway. That'll get me through this.

I stop at the mailbox on the way out: more bills. Lets see If I owe anything yet. Nope, I still have some credit. Oh, good, the checks I ordered are here too. Nothing else though? Really? It's fine, I don't want cards from people anyway.

Parking at the grocery store, I notice Pinky's across the street looks abandoned, but I guess all bars appear that way during the day. I'm glad, that means I won't run into Deanna.

Inside, I'm pushing one cart while dragging another behind me. I want to get enough canned food and non-perishable stuff like toilet paper and soap to last longer than my last trip did. Ooh, the bakery! I detour to pick up a box of doughnuts to eat while I shop and I'll pay for them with the empty container. That's not illegal right? Eh, I don't really care right now.

In the canned food aisle, I've eaten three doughnuts and already have one cart filled up with the same old junk I bought last time when a woman's voice says, "May!" and I'm embraced in her arms.

What the hell? It's freaking Brenda!

She says, "I was just picking up some things then I

was going to come see you. Surprise!"

It's a surprise all right. "What are you doing here?"

"Well, I wanted to give you some time to yourself, but since you won't talk to me over the phone, I thought I should check in on you. It's nice to see you out and about, you wouldn't believe what I imagined."

"I'm fine."

She smiles and nods. "I like your outfit."

Seriously? She must need something. No one compliments someone on dirty shorts and a tank top with flowers on them. I grab more cans off the shelves and finish stocking one of my carts.

"Are you throwing yourself a birthday party or preparing for the end of the world?"

She's always reminding me of my freaking birthday... I guess it's May already. I didn't think I spent that much time waiting for Limpy, and if it has been that long, then maybe he really is never coming back.

I push and drag my carts down the aisle away from her.

"Can I help you with that?"

"No." She's probably following me anyway.

"So, whatcha been up to?"

"Same old." I knew it, I knew she was following me.

"Well, congratulations on buying a house and car. That's a big step."

Gah! I hadn't thought of it like that, and I would rather not think of it at all. She knows just how to get under my skin. I keep moving.

"I've kept up your house for you, so...you're welcome."

I stop abruptly. "Why are you really here?"

"Uh, I told you. I wanted to check on you, make sure you're doing okay here in your millionaire Florida life, that's all."

Oh, I see. I bet she's out of money. Why else would she say millionaire? Money never crosses my mind, especially not the settlement, until I have to and she's probably been thinking about it every single day. Well, she's not getting any of it. I fill my second cart with paper products and soap then move on and add a couple cases of bottled water.

"May?"

"I said I'm fine! You came, you saw, now you can leave."

"C'mon. I flew all this way. I want to see where you're living so I don't worry so much. I mean, I saw some pictures online, but—"

"Oh, so you can move in here too? What'd you do, burn my other house down?"

"No. Jeez. Don't be so defensive. You're my sister, and sisters keep up with each other, especially when…you know."

"When my family dies?"

"Yes—But *I'm* still your family too."

"Whatever." I walk away from her, leaving my carts behind. All she wants is money, I just know it. She's a terrible liar.

As I walk out the door she hollers at me. I walk faster to my car. If I can make it to the house before her, then I can lock her out. Maybe then she'll understand I neither want or need her company. She doesn't get it, that she's changed since my Annie passed. She's ruined our relationship.

Back at the house, Limpy is on the porch. I

saunter up to him. "Well, well, well. Look who it is."

"Keow. Keow."

"As well you should be sorry! Do you know how worried I've been?"

"Krrr."

"Okay, you're forgiven." I open the front door, "Come one, let's go inside." He follows me in.

Trying my best not to scare him, since he's walking slow and cocking his head to look around, I shut and lock the door. This works out great! My bird is safely locked in, and Brenda is locked out.

I sit on the futon in the living room, "So...guess who followed me to Florida? My sister. Can you believe it?"

"Keow. Keow." He's inspecting the fake palm tree in the corner.

"So what? She's annoying and I don't have to like her just because she's my sister."

He turns to me, "Krrr-eeeow!"

"We'll see. I think she's after money, but you might be right. I still don't see how I can have a relationship with her again after how she's ben acting."

"Krrr-eeeow! Keow! Keow!"

"Excuse me? I have a reason!"

He walks into the dining room, then disappears into the kitchen.

I follow him, "Did I ever tell you my husband and daughter are dead and now I'm alone? That's my reason."

He flies past me and lands on the dining table.

"It's traumatic! I mean, look at me. Look at you. We're having a conversation...I feel kind of silly now."

"Krrr-eeeow!"

"You're right. My Annie used to talk to animals,

and it wasn't anything crazy. But it's cute when kids do it. If anyone saw me, well I'd be locked up for sure. That almost happened once already, did I tell you that?"

"Keow."

"No, I don't need help. I'm fine until I die."

"Keow. Keow." He jumps off the table and runs into my bedroom.

I sit at the dining table. "Don't poop on my bed!"

He flies back into the living room, lands on the floor and runs over to me. "Keow! Keow!"

"Oh, ok." He must want a snack. "Hang on, I'll be right back." I sneak out the door and go down to the water's edge and search. I thought there were supposed to be lots of those apple snails around, but now I can't find any. I mosey along until I find one then head back to the house.

There's a car parked next to mine, then I hear, "Shoo!" and Limpy flies over my head.

I drop the snail and run to the porch. "Brenda? What the hell!"

She spins around to face me, "Oh, hey, I got all your groceries for you. Did you know there was a bird *inside* your house?"

"You scared him away!"

"Yeah? You don't like birds. I was trying to help."

"Well, you're not helping! Don't you get it? I moved down here to get away from you! You ruin everything!"

"Me?" She shakes her head and walks toward her car where she grabs a few grocery bags then brings them onto the porch. "I've only ever been supportive of you," She goes back to the car then returns with more groceries. "I've made sacrifices for you. To be there for you." She makes one last trip to the car and comes back, "And not once have you said thank you. Not once."

"Nobody asked you to help."

She snaps, "You don't *need* to ask me! We're family."

I roll my eyes.

She hugs me, "I'm trying my best to be supportive. Damn it, I may not always get it right, but I'm trying."

Maybe she has a point. Am I not appreciating the things she's done that were actually helpful? I try to think back, but I can't help focussing on all the times I told her to go away and she wouldn't leave, which isn't helpful at all in my opinion. People need their space. It shouldn't be up to me to explain this to her. If she really cared, then she would just know.

She sighs. "Here's the receipt for your groceries. You can write a check if you don't have cash."

"Ah-ha! I knew it! You need money."

"Yes—no. I mean, yes I need money for the groceries, but I'm not here to get money from you. How could you think that?"

"Because the settlement is all you ever talk about."

"That's not true, and you know it."

"Do I?"

"Well I would hope so. I'm not rich, but I certainly can't afford to buy your doomsday groceries after the plane ticket down here to check on you. Who else is checking on you, huh? Who else cares?"

"My bird, Limpy. He cares."

"Oh? Is the bird going to make sure your bills are paid? Is the bird going to call emergency services if you die here?"

"I pay my bills! I'm not a freaking child, Brenda!"

"Then quit acting like one!"

We stare at each other in silence. Then she goes and gets the rest of the groceries from her car while I start bringing the bags from the porch inside.

CHAPTER SIXTEEN

Introductions

Brenda started a load of my laundry in the washing machine, and is now making lunch. I'm curious if being in Florida will influence her cooking at all.

Nope. But I can't blame her, all she had to work with is the junk I had in my carts at the grocery store. She did burn the canned pasta a little, but I've burned it too, so I can't blame her for that either.

There's plenty of Limpkins crying outside, but none are close enough to be Limpy. I hope she didn't scare him away for good. She's got no sense about her anymore since Annie died.

She says, "I'm sleeping here tonight."

I shrug because it's the middle of the day and

there's plenty of time for her to change her mind.

"Do you have any wine?"

I shrug again.

"I'll run back up to the store and get some, and I'll pick up some real groceries too." She holds out her hand.

"What?"

"I need money for the groceries and wine."

Ugh. Wine does sound good though. I check my wallet then hand her a twenty dollar bill.

Her hand is still out. I give her another twenty, then another, and now that's apparently enough. She puts the cash in her pocket, grabs her keys and is out the door before I can think of anything snarky to say.

I stand on the porch and holler to her as she's getting in her car, "Red wine! Not white."

"Duh!" She says. Then she shuts her door and drives off.

When the dust settles, I look around for Limpy, but I think I know it'll be a while before I see him again.

I lay on the living room floor awaiting Brenda's eventual return. At least I know she's coming back, rather than being surprised again. And I guess it's okay if she sleeps here tonight. It sounds like she's broke, so I would be a bad person if I sent her out to a motel she can't afford.

There's a knock at the door.

Why is she knocking? So freaking annoying. I heave myself up off the floor and open the door.

It's Luis. He's holding a paper plate covered in tinfoil, and a gift bag. "Hi, May!"

Did I not get the memo that today is the day to 'stop by and visit May'?

"My daughters made cupcakes, so I thought I

125

would bring you one and see how you are settling in since I never heard from you during the holidays—which I completely understand. Holidays are tough for me too."

I let him inside and take the plate. "Yeah, thanks."

He continues, "Then, I saw this in that clothing store we went to together and I thought of you. Hope you like it." He hands me the bag.

"How did you know my birthday?"

"Aw, it's your birthday today? What a wonderful coincidence!"

"I don't know if it's today, but my sister showed up and mentioned it. So, it's sometime around now."

"I see," he says, though clearly he doesn't. "You never mentioned a sister."

"She's living up north, in my house."

"Aw, and she came down to visit you for your birthday? Well, she must be special, like you for letting her live there."

I squint at him. "You know, you don't have to keep checking in on me, or bring me any gifts."

"Oh, it's the least I can do for a friend. The van is such a blessing too, runs perfectly and the girls love it. It makes life much easier. I think of you every time I drive it."

Great. I set the plate on the side table then sit on the futon to open the gift bag. It's another track suit, but this one is pink. Not my favorite color, but if it's as comfortable as the purple suit, then I'm happy with it. "Thank you."

"I'm glad you like it." He smiles. "So, how have you been doing?"

"Fine, until today."

"What happened?"

"Well—"

Brenda fumbles in the front door with her hands full of grocery bags, then stops when she notices Luis, who is also seemingly awstruck. Then she sets the bags on the dining table and straightens her shirt.

He tidies himself too as he walks over to her, his hand extended. "Hi. I'm Luis, you must be May's sister?"

I stay sitting on the futon.

Her cheeks flush bright pink as she places her hand in his. "Brenda. Nice to meet you. How do you two know each other?"

"At first I was the realtor, but we've become friends."

She looks at me, "Friends?"

Luis pipes in, "Yes. *Just* friends."

Both of them giggle then she says, "I understand, I'm just surprised May opened up to anyone. Do you know…?"

"Yes, we've talked about her family."

"Really?"

"I'm in a similar situation myself. I lost my wife a few years ago."

"Oh, I'm so sorry…"

Pfft! Is that a glimmer of joy in her eyes?

Brenda jumps, "Oh, shoot, I have more groceries in the car."

Luis says, "I'll help you."

As soon as the door shuts behind them, I sneak over to the dining room window. He's holding her hand to help her down the steps. Now he's letting her carry one bag in each hand while he handles all the rest. They both have wide, goofy looking smiles on their faces.

Shit, they're coming back. I run and sit back down

on the futon, unwrap the cupcake and bite off half of it so it looks like I never got up.

They enter, and neither even glances at me. Rude. I hear them unpacking and putting all the groceries away in the kitchen. I finish my cupcake.

Then they come into the living room and Brenda hands me a small gift bag and says, "Happy Birthday."

I pull the tissue paper out, then unravel it. It's a small rectangular refrigerator magnet. I flip it over and on the front there's a painted picture of green rolling hills, blue sky with puffy white clouds, a rainbow and some birds flying. In the sky under the rainbow it says: A woman without her sister is like a bird without wings.

Hm. I think about it for a minute.

"Do you like it?"

"Yeah." I'm not sure if I do though. I mean, it's cute, but why would she get me a bird quote magnet when she knows I don't really like birds, except Limpy who she chased away? She never makes sense.

Luis says, "What a thoughtful gift."

I set the magnet with the pink track suit next to me, then stand up in between them so they quit smiling at each other. It's not that I don't want them to like each other, but they can do it on their own time.

Then, as if he heard me, he says, "Well, I better get going. Let you two have your sister time."

Brenda says, "Oh, no, please. Stay for a glass of wine. Do you like wine?"

"I do." He looks at me, his eyes full of hope.

How can I say no? I'm out numbered. I can't get any freaking peace anyway. "I'll take a glass."

She steps closer toward Luis and, in his excitement, he hugs her. Then when the hug is over, she leans toward the couch to grab the magnet she got me, "I was just going to put this on the fridge."

He says, "Oh, I'm sorry, I thought—"

"No, please, don't be sorry. I love hugs."

They giggle and go into the kitchen.

I follow but lean against the dining room wall with my arms folded. I don't want to go in because they're flirting like teenagers. They're taking forever too. I want my wine now more than ever. I thought it would be interesting to sit back and watch them, but it's another reminder of how happy everyone is despite how I'm feeling. Honestly? It's rude.

Finally I get my wine and sit on the porch. Then they come out too, but they'll need to bring one dining chair out for them both to have a place to sit.

Luis says to Brenda, "Has May shown you the property yet?"

"Not yet. I just got in today."

He asks me, "We could show her now, if you're up to it."

I wave my hand, "You know it better than me. Go ahead."

They walk down off the porch and around the side of the house. I can still kind of hear them.

She says, "Are there alligators?"

"Absolutely! But, don't worry, I will protect you."

Then their conversation becomes indistinct.

Where the hell is Limpy? I want his company so bad right now. I guess so I'm not a third wheel, which is somehow more lonesome than being alone. I slowly finish my drink, mosey inside for a refill, then resume sitting in my seat on the porch.

A while later Brenda and Luis come back, and

they're holding hands. Seriously? What'd they do, make out behind the house? Why are they stopped by the stairs?

Brenda says, "Oh, May!" Like she didn't expect me to still be outside in the heat, "We're meeting up at Pinky's later. They're putting on some kind of show. Want to come?"

"No."

"Come on, you have to come."

I fold my arms.

"I better go," says Luis, "I have to feed the munchkins and make sure my sister is okay with watching them tonight. I'm sure she'll understand." He turns to Brenda, "Hope to see you later," and kisses her on the cheek.

Her dreamy gaze is fixed on him as he gets in his car and drives down the driveway and out of sight. Then she turns to me, "Okay, birthday girl, lets get you cleaned up for your night out. I picked you up a couple of razors at the store so you can shave those hairy legs of yours." She goes into the kitchen.

I run my hand down my leg. Yeah, I probably could use a shave. But who says I'm going out with her? If I stay here, I wouldn't have to get cleaned up or shave. "I'm not going," I pour myself some more wine.

"Oh, you're coming."

"Why? So I can sit there while you guys fondle each other? No thanks."

"For your birthday."

"Right."

She puts her hand on mine, "Okay, so I *also* want to spend more time with him. C'mon, May, I've never felt a spark like that. You see it too, right? Can't you do it for me as a thanks for everything I've done for you?"

"He's got three daughters," I pull my hand free from hers and count on my fingers, "one, two, three. And they're young."

"I know, he told me. Honestly? It's a perfect situation for me since I never got to have any."

"What if he leaves you after you bond with them and you never get to see them again? And what if one of them dies? Do you know how much it hurts?"

"Of course I do. I lost Annie too ya'know." Her eyes well up. "You had a child, so you don't know what it's like to want kids and never have any."

I clench my fists, "You're right. I *had* a child, who *just* died. You're so insensitive!"

"May…it's been a couple years now…"

Years? I shake my head. No. I don't believe it.

"You turned forty-five the year she went to camp. How old are you now?"

"I'm…" I try to do the math.

"You're forty-seven."

"Two years? That's not a long time. You can't rush me!" I hear myself say these words, but I still can't believe it's been years at all, months maybe, but surely not years. She must be lying.

She continues, "I loved Annie like she was my own, and I'm still hurting too, but I've found a sense of peace in knowing she's an angel now. I'm thankful for the time I had with her, and I'm sure you are too. Nothing will fill that void and we will never forget her, or Dave, but they would want us to be happy. I feel like Luis could be *the one* for me."

I. Can't. Process. This.

"Wouldn't you want—"

"Stop it! Just stop it! You don't know what you're talking about!"

"Can you please—"

I cover my ears with my hands and sing, "Lalalalala."

She grabs a hold of my arms to pull them down.

Pacing around the room with my ears still covered, thoughts race in my mind. How could that much time have passed? Ugh, I feel like I'm being hit with the news all over again.

When I turn around, Brenda is standing in front of me, holding out a glass of water.

"I don't want water!" I smack the cup out of her hand and it flies across the room, just missing the rug, and shatters on the wood floor. "Go away! Leave me alone!"

She's standing there, wide-eyed and frozen.

"Get out! Get out!" I stomp my feet, "Get out of my house!"

She grabs her keys and walks out the door.

CHAPTER SEVENTEEN

Searching For Peace

It's night now and I still can't calm down. Brenda hasn't returned since I yelled at her, and I have to admit a small part of me feels bad about that. At least she listened for once, but damn it, I was making progress until she came to town. Everything was manageable, my grief was manageable.

Am I the butt of some cosmic joke? She follows me to Florida and all of a sudden it's been years since my Annie died? Where did the time go? Ugh! I can't stand this and I certainly can't handle it.

I finish the bottle of wine opened earlier. My head is a little fuzzy and my stomach a little tingly, but it's not enough. I want to be numb.

I'm looking in the kitchen, but I don't see the other bottles, and I know she bought more than one. They have to be here somewhere. Maybe she tried to hide them from me in the back of a cabinet. I open them all and start pulling stuff out until the counters are full, then I let stuff fall onto the floor. No wine. Gah! She's so annoying.

Hm…Oh! Maybe she put them in the refrigerator. I check. Of course she did. There they are, three glorious bottles. I put them on the dining table. Damn, the corkscrew is in that mess in the kitchen somewhere.

I'll figure it out. I try to open a bottle with my keys, digging out bits of cork. Then I try a knife, but now what's left of the cork is inside the bottle. Oh well, I pour the wine into my glass from earlier and drink it down. I'm pretty sure I swallowed some cork too. Is that how God is going to take me? The cork is going to get lodged somewhere in my body and I'll explode? That'll be a good parting gift from me to Brenda.

Bleh, Brenda, Brenda, Brenda. I can't even stand her name anymore. It doesn't even rhyme with anything. She's got some nerve blurting out how long my daughter has been dead, like I want to know!

One time, back when my husband was still alive— apparently many years ago now— I told her in confidence that I had won a thousand dollars on a two dollar scratch-off ticket, and Annie and I were going to surprise Dave with it when he got home. Well, she ruined it and I could've strangled her. Did I yell at her? No, because it's not like she did it on purpose. One of those innocent mistakes I guess.

Of course, that time was nothing compared to when she told the whole world I was finally pregnant, robbing me of the chance to share the news myself. She swore I told her it was okay, but why would I do that? And did I even get upset with her? No. She's my little sister, so she always gets a pass. She never had family of her own, and we always included her anyway.

Little sister or not, we're both grown women. She needs to live her own life and quit ruining mine. Yeah, we used to be close and yeah, we had good times, but things have changed damn it!

I need to read Annie's letter to get my sister out of my brain. I stumble into the dark bedroom, bump into the night table, and the lamp falls onto the floor. Whatever, I don't need light. I feel around and find the letter, my framed family picture, the angel necklace and the peace rock, then bring everything out onto the dining table.

I set it all up in front of me like a shrine, illuminated in the yellowish light from the ugly brass chandelier looming above me, then stare at all of it while drinking down another glass of wine. The rock is out of place. I'm never going to find peace. I clutch it in my fist, stomp outside next to the tree then throw it as far as I can. It plops into water. That's better.

Now I'm acutely aware of how dark it is out here. Who knows what's lurking around, waiting to pounce on me. I try to run back inside, but running is hard so I speed-walk instead. It's effective.

Back inside, looking at my family picture without the stupid rock in the way, I remember what a beautiful family I had. Why did this happen to me? Of all the people in the world, why me? Why them? I kiss Dave and Annie, then stroke the frame with my finger. I'm still justified in my grieving. Everyone's different. I finish another glass of wine. The picture is becoming blurry. I better read Annie's letter now while I still can.

A tear rolls down my cheek. She was such a good daughter, better than I deserved. So wise for her years, and strong enough to care for me when I had a bad day after Dave died. He was her father, and she was probably hurting too, but she was stronger than me, I think. Yes, she definitely was. I was lucky, and now I'm in hell. I pour another glass and sip on it. They were my angels, saving me from this wretched life, and now they're gone.

"Why, God? Why did you take them from me?"

No answer.

Ugh. This bottle is done, time to open another one. I used the same method as before: dig out as much cork as I can then push the rest of it into the liquid.

I start reading the letter from the beginning. This is hard. I can't tell if the room is spinning or if it's my vision. Maybe my eyeballs are rolling around.

A bright spot of light catches my eye, at the top of the page, right over the—There's a date! I bring the letter closer to my face, then move it away again to try to focus. I don't believe it. No, Brenda must have written that. But it's in Annie's handwriting…What year is it now?

Something in this house has to have the date on it. I rummage but can't find a damn thing. Oh! The house paperwork! Where is it? Oh, it's in the car. I don't know if I can make it that far now I'm on my second bottle of wine, but I have to. I have to know.

I shuffle my way out to my car and fall in the driver's seat. I lean over to finger through the glove compartment. Here it is. Where's the date? Where's the date? Shit. It can't be! I jump out of the car, leaving the door open, and hurry back into the house with the paperwork. It can't be. It can't be. I down the rest of my drink like a shot of tequila, take a deep breath, then compare the date to Annie's letter.

She was right. Freaking Brenda was freaking right it's been two freaking years! I scream at the top of my lungs to release this pressure in my chest. My heart feels like a sink hole and the rest of my body is caving into it.

What have I done in two years? Is that a long time to grieve? Pfft. I'll probably grieve them for the rest of my life, which, God willing, will be short.

I grab a can of beans off the kitchen floor and throw it into the living room. It bounces softly on the futon. Damn it. I get another can, march into the living room and throw it at the fake palm tree. It hits the wall but doesn't damage anything. Stupid tree! I scream and lunge at it, crumpling the top leaves in my fists until I wrestle it to the ground. Then I kick it.

What else can I destroy? I pull the futon mattress half off the frame, but it's so heavy! Then I hurl a dining chair at the futon. There. Much better.

No it's not. None of this makes me feel better. My family is still dead! I clench my fists and scream at the ceiling, "I hate this!"

"Krrr-eeeow! Keow! Keow! Keow! Keow!"

"Limpy?" I run out onto the porch, "Oh Limpy! You came back!"

"Keow! Keow!"

"What's wrong is my Dave and Annie are dead."

"Keow!"

"I'm all alone…"

"Keow. Keow. Keow."

"But I am!" My eyes well up.

"Krrr-eeeow!"

"I don't know how to live now. This isn't my life. This isn't me. I'm not some single, middle-aged woman— I don't even have a hobby! What am I supposed to do now? I was born to be a wife and a mother. I don't know if I can love again, and I can't have another baby. I'm supposed to have grandkids to keep me busy in my old age. I'm supposed to have Dave growing old with me so we can laugh at each other's wrinkled butts like we planned."

"Krrr-eeeow!"

"Yeah? And who would let me adopt a child?" I point at myself, "I'm a wreck! I can't even take care of myself."

"Keow. Keow."

"Brenda? Please, I don't want to talk about her."

"Krrr." He's walking away.

"Where are you going? Stay with me!" He's only a brown blur now. I crawl to follow him, and tumble down the steps.

Scrambling to my feet in the yard I scream, "Limpy!" into the blackness of the night.

Then I notice the stars. My vision is so slow and blurred they look like bright streaks, like each one is a shooting star. It's so beautiful... I stand here, my body swaying.

I'm warm all of a sudden, like a heated blanket has been wrapped around me. "God, is that you?" A sense of peace—just a sense of it, enters my mind. It feels so good. Brenda was right about the dates so she's probably right that Dave and Annie would want me to be happy.

The peace rock! It's in the water, but I know I can find it... I have to, to find my peace. Putting one foot in front of the other I plod along toward the marsh. The ground becomes squishy. I'm close. I drop to my hands and knees and start feeling around.

It's here somewhere. A little bit further into the water maybe? Here it is! Yes! I've found it at last! I laugh and cry, clutching it in my hands against my chest. I'm never letting it go.

I try to stand up but I fall right back down to my knees. Crawling is too hard. I inch forward, rolling from my stomach to my side and pushing my knees against the earth, toward the house until I'm out of the muck.

On solid ground, I roll over onto my back so I can see the stars with my newfound peace. My heart is beating strong, and I'm so warm. I laugh some more, then close my eyes.

CHAPTER EIGHTEEN

Realizations

"Ma'am, can you hear me?"

I open my eyes but everything is blurry. It's some guy standing over me.

He continues, "Are you hurt?"

"What?" I sit up.

"Follow my finger," he says, moving his index finger back and forth in front of my face.

"Oh, my head."

"Where does your head hurt?"

I blink my eyes and can see this guy is a paramedic, so I clarify, "Too much wine."

Then he calls out, "She's over here! She's okay. No stretcher."

Why is there a paramedic? He helps me to my feet where I notice all the flashing lights of the ambulance and police cars, and a bunch of people all in front of my house.

"Where is my peace? I was holding a rock that said peace, where is it?"

He squints at me, places his hand on my shoulder and says, "Ma'am, you were holding a snail."

Shit. How much wine did I drink?

"Would you like to talk to a therapist? We can—"

"No. I'm fine."

Making my way toward the house, I put my hands over my face to block out the light of day and flashing lights. I'm sunburned, and caked with dirt. Maybe it was all a dream. A stupid drunken dream.

I peek through my fingers in time to see Brenda running up to me.

She wraps her arms around me, "Oh, May! I thought something terrible happened. I came to check on you and your car was open, your house was torn apart, and I couldn't find you anywhere. I thought you were abducted! Or—or murdered! Oh, I'm so glad you're okay, I don't know what I would do without you!"

Why would I, of all people, be abducted?

Then Luis says, "We were so worried about you."

Are the two of them 'we' already?

"Damn, pussycat! Rough night?" says a familiar voice.

Ugh, it's Deanna.

I look around at the crowd. No one else I recognize. Besides these three they're all strangers doing their jobs. They'll probably all go home and tell their families about the crazy lady they rescued from the marsh. Some might even add that they fought off an alligator. I probably would if I were them.

The paramedic ushers me over to an ambulance. Brenda, Luis and Deanna follow like little ducklings.

"Just need to get you checked out," the paramedic says.

I'm poked and prodded and made to follow, with my eyes, more fingers moving back and forth in front of my face. Then I'm handed a gatorade and an aspirin. Don't they have anything stronger? Oh well.

The ambulance and police cars drive away and I'm left with the three poor souls who think they actually care about me. I'm sure they don't. For the love birds, I'm their common link right now, and their reason to see each other. And Deanna? She's just weird.

We all go inside. They apparently want to make *extra* sure that I'm okay. So annoying. This is the first time I really want to take a shower. Maybe they'll be gone when I get out.

I start the shower then get a good look at myself in the bathroom mirror. I'm a crusty old lady who failed at giving herself a mud mask. Guess I'm lucky they found me when they did. I'm not as sunburned as I feel. What time is it? Eh, it doesn't matter.

Oh, this shower is so nice. The water is a perfect temperature and I have soap! Do Dave and Annie have to shower in Heaven? Probably not, or only if they want to.

I put on my pink track suit, then flop on the bed, listening to the muffled conversations on the other side of the wall. Obviously they're not gone like I hoped. Unless this is another mind trick?

There's a knock at my bedroom door. "How're you coming along in there?" asks Brenda.

Okay, it's not a mind trick. Guess I better get up. They're not going to leave until they see me all cleaned up, so they did their duty. It's kind of nice, now that I think about it, to know people cared enough to check on me, but I still want them to go away. Maybe I am crazy? Complaining for company then wanting them to leave…

They're all smiling at me when I open the door. Normal people might smile back, but I'm too hungover. Stupid aspirin needs to start working.

I go to the kitchen, open the fridge and stick my head inside while leaning on the door. Nothing's appetizing, but the coolness is soothing on my face.

"You know what you need, pussycat?" says Deanna, "A Bloody Mary and a nice greasy cheeseburger."

"Stop calling me pussycat." A burger does sound good though.

"Meow," she swipes her hand in the air like a cat's paw.

I shake my head and move on to the cupboards. If I can find something as good as a burger sounds then I don't have to go anywhere. Deanna is standing behind me, I just know it. She has a presence about her I guess, like you couldn't miss her in a crowd if she were invisible. I grab a can of beans and turn around to try and imagine how it might taste. Warm, lumpy—bleh! Beans aren't going to work.

She says, "No, you don't want to eat that. You want a cheeeeeseburger…at Piiiiinky's…"

Damn it, she's right, my mouth is watering and I can almost taste it.

"They have a show this afternoon. Starts in a little bit actually, and I bet you'd like it."

I'm thinking.

Brenda and Luis come into the kitchen too, which can barely hold us all, and Brenda says, "Did I hear someone say Pinky's? That's a great idea!"

I shrug.

Deanna says, "They make the best burgers in town."

"I'd love to go," Luis says, "I happen to be kid-free for the rest of the day. They stayed with my sister-in-law last night and she's taking them to the water-park in Orlando today. What do you say, May?"

"I don't want to celebrate my birthday."

Brenda sighs, "Fine. Then lets go for no reason."

I tap my finger on the can of beans.

"It'll be good for you."

Yeah, like she knows what's good for me. I slam the can of beans on the counter.

"All right. You know what? If you don't come out with us, I'm moving in."

Freaking great. I bet she would do it too, she's done it before. But if she moves into this place, I can go back to my house up north. Hm…Annoying neighbors, lawn to mow, and memories—too many memories. I don't think I can do it, and moreso, I don't think I *want* to. Is that terrible of me?

She continues, "I'm serious. There's nothing for me up there anymore. Down here I have you and," she wraps her arms around Luis, "wonderful new beginnings."

Gah! She's like a parasite. Everywhere I go, she's there, crawling under my skin, invading my life.

Deanna says, "Aw, that's sweet."

Why is she still here?

Luis says, "You know, it's not my place to say, but

from what Brenda tells me, and from what you've told me, it might be good for you to have some fun. I wish I had this kind of support after my wife passed."

No, it's not his place. I don't need to be ganged up on in my own house.

Brenda pulls a paper from her purse and holds it up to me. It's the stub of her plane ticket—her *one-way* plane ticket.

I say, "You planned it this way!"

"I planned to come see you, and I couldn't afford the roundtrip." She grins. "It's just working out."

"So you *do* need money."

"Yes, but that's not the only reason. You need help. Every time I leave you alone for a while you get hurt."

"Seriously? You're such a—you really just—UGH!" What I meant to say was I get hurt every time she pops in on me. It's her fault.

Everyone is quiet which gives me a minute to ponder things. If Brenda can't afford the round trip plane ticket, she's staying anyway. —Wait, she's lying. Of course she could afford it.

I ask, "Then where did you stay last night? And how did you pay for it?"

"Well…" she winks at Luis and his cheeks flush.

"That's fast. So, move in with him."

"May."

"What?"

"Come on. Don't be like that."

"Like what? I'm not the one who's changed."

"Is that so?"

"Yeah. You're annoying as hell now and I can't stand to be around you. All you do is ruin everything!"

She turns to Luis, "See? This is what I'm talking

about. She—"

I snap, "Don't talk about me like I'm not here! I'm right freaking here!"

"May, do you even know where you'd be without me? Probably homeless, or stuck in that psych ward of the hospital. I mean, you don't even know half of the stuff I've done for you. But, you know what? Say what you want, I know you don't mean it. It's fine. You're my sister and I love you. I always will, no matter what."

"Psych ward huh?" says Deanna.

"I don't need this." I go sit on the floor in the living room.

A moment later they all come in and Brenda says, "We just want you to have some fun. That's all. We can talk about the rest another time."

Deanna sings, "Cheeeeseburgers!"

My stomach is growling at me. "Fine! If it'll get you all off my back."

CHAPTER NINETEEN

Or Else!

Heading to Pinky's, I'm stuck in the back of Luis' van with Deanna like a child while 'mom and dad' are up front. Deanna keeps trying to talk to me, even though I'm turned in my seat so my back is facing her. Maybe she just has no concept of boundaries or something.

A thought occurs to me. I turn toward her, "Why were you at my house anyway?"

"Oh, I'm a volunteer rescuer, didn't I tell you that?"

There's lots of things she probably told me that I tuned out.

"Yeah, I've had some EMT training, some alligator training, assisted some searches and all that. So when I heard the call for a possible search and rescue by the marsh at your address, I figured I'd help."

Hm. Makes sense.

"I thought you'd been eaten actually. Thought I'd be finding your hairy legs lying in the bushes somewhere." She laughs, "I was gonna take 'em home as a souvenir."

I'm not amused.

We arrive at Pinky's. Must be a popular show, the parking lot is so full we have to park on the side street. I was hoping we would be the only ones attending so I didn't have to deal with a crowd.

Deanna checks her watch. "Perfect. Just enough time to get food before the show starts."

Ah, yes, food. Must have food.

Inside, the place is loud with thumping music and it's crowded, but we still manage to find seats at a small round table in the back. Why did they bring me here when they know my head is killing me? What's the point of any of this? We won't even be able to see the show from here. At least there won't be much talking. I can hardly hear myself think.

I'm sitting at the table with Brenda and Luis on my left, who are still absorbed in each other, then Deanna's on my right. It's like I'm here as her date. Ugh.

A young male dressed in suspenders, but no shirt, takes our orders. I have to yell that I want a bloody Mary, a cheeseburger and a basket of fries, exactly what I came for. I can practically taste it.

When I look at my sister flirting with my realtor I want to gag. Instead I try to remember the peace I felt last night. But now I just feel angry because I didn't find my peace or the stupid rock. Another cosmic joke I'm sure.

Did I even really want it? It did feel good while I had it, but I hate being bamboozled like that. Hm. I like that word, and it makes sense because I had so much booze. I guess I was asking to be made a fool of.

I turn my head slightly toward Deanna who says to me, "So, Luis said you were going through some rough times, losing your family and all. How's the recovery goin'?"

Recovery? Seriously? "They're dead." She's terrible at small talk.

She speaks louder, "Yeah, I know. I mean *your* recovery. Grieving."

"Oh, I dunno."

"Well, in my opinion, you're doing a bang up job."

What does that even mean? I assume it's good because she's giving me a thumbs up.

"So, pussycat—"

"Stop calling me that."

"All right, all right. You ever been to a show like this?"

I squint my eyes. I think she said snow, but then I put it together in my head. How would I know? I don't even know what kind of show this is supposed to be.

She continues, "A drag show."

"What?"

Then my drink arrives, garnished with two green olives, a piece of shrimp and a celery stalk. I take a gulp then eat the shrimp. So good.

Deanna holds her glass up in the middle of the table and says, "Cheers!"

Brenda and Luis clink their glasses against hers, then each others, and now all three of them are waiting on me. I raise my glass. They all clink theirs against mine and say cheers again. Such a stupid thing to do. Just drink your drink. There's another word they should find an alternative to. Why do so many words have double meanings?

"Oh shit," Deanna leans close to me and whispers, "You see that chick over there? That's my ex, the one I told you about that stole my car."

I can't help but look. The woman has short pink hair and is wearing some kind of white overalls that are shorts instead of pants. She's holding hands with some other woman with tattoos and long brown hair pulled back in a low pony tail.

Deanna says, "Can you believe that? What a ho."

"Well, you picked her."

"For the record, she presented herself as a stable-Mable and not this lyin', cheatin' Debbie-do-all."

I keep a straight face, but I'm laughing on the inside. I must be really old to not know all these funny ways to describe things.

I ask, "How old are you?"

"Forty-seven."

Hm. "Me too."

"So…wanna pretend to be my girlfriend so I can get a little revenge?"

"No."

"C'mon. I'd do it for you." She pokes my side.

"No." She doesn't even know me. I'd rather the town not know me either, and I certainly don't want to get mixed up in any drama.

Finally my food arrives. I grab the cheeseburger in both hands. It's bursting with meat, cheese, lettuce and tomato and I shove it into my mouth to take a bite. So. Good.

The lights dim, the audience applauds, and a spotlight shines on a shimmery gold curtain against the far wall opposite us. Then the music stops and the people are quiet. A very tall, muscular woman emerges in an emerald green sequined dress, what is obviously a red wig and way too much makeup. "Hello, hello, everyone! For those who don't know me, I'm Miss Ruby Love." The audience hoots, hollers and whistles. "Thank you. Thank you. I'll be your host this evening and we have a fabulous show in store for all you ladies and gents and in-betweens. First up we have a newcomer to the scene. Please welcome that sweet drop of chocolate, Coco LaRain!"

These can't be their real names. I can't even comprehend what kind of show this is going to be. I shove a few fries in my mouth.

Ruby leaves the stage and I assume this is Coco, a woman with huge breasts in a blue frilly gown adorned in crystals. A song starts playing and Coco starts singing. Or is she? Nope, she's mouthing the words, though she's doing a pretty good job. They could stand to turn the volume down a notch.

Deanna says, "Awesome, right?"

I nod as I suck on the straw to my drink. I'm not really paying attention. From what I saw, they're at least pretty enough to be on a stage.

"Want to come up with me?"

"For what?"

"To give her a tip." She holds up a dollar bill to me then hollers over me, "You guys goin' up?"

Brenda giggles. That's a no. Luis pulls out a dollar and hands it over to Deanna. I didn't bring any cash, so I can't go up anyway, not that I even would.

She makes her way toward the stage then disappears into the crowd. A moment later she emerges, coming back toward us with a smile on her face. Something good must've happened.

I finish my burger by the time the next performer gets on stage, a large woman with brown hair teased out and hair-sprayed like a helmet, dressed in a shiny yellow dress with a long train. I didn't understand her name. Betty Lemondrop? Who cares anymore. I can't keep track.

Halfway through the song I've finished my fries and most of my drink.

Deanna hands me a dollar and says, "I'll buy your next drink if you go give this to Betty."

Hm. I could use another to get through this, but I can buy my own damn drink. I shake my head.

She starts chanting, "Do it. Do it. Do it."

Brenda says, "Yes, you should totally do it! It'll be good for you."

"No!"

"Do it, or else!"

She can't add on to her original threat, that's not fair.

"I said, or else! Get up there."

I snatch the dollar and start walking toward the stage. There's so many people I don't think I'll even make it. I turn around and the crowd clears to make a perfect line of sight from me to Deanna, Brenda and Luis, who are all staring at me, hooting and hollering.

A little closer to Betty, I'd swear she's a man. But some women are built like that, I try not to judge, especially when I'm in a pink track suit.

I hold out the dollar and Betty, while not breaking character or song, winks at me with her super long eyelashes, caresses my arm, and takes the bill. I smile at her and I don't know why. It's like I'm nervous or something, and my cheeks even feel warm. I hurry back to my seat and try to straighten my face so no one notices. There's a fresh drink waiting for me at the table, so I start drinking it.

Then the song ends and Miss Ruby Love comes back on stage. Apparently she's the final performance. Good. I'm ready to leave now that I'm full, plus I've fulfilled what I said so Brenda doesn't move in with me. Don't get me wrong, I'm having an okay time, but I don't want to linger once the show is done.

Deanna dangles another dollar in front of me.

"No, I did one, that's enough. You give your own money."

"Fine, I will." Deanna walks up into the crowd, then all of a sudden the people scatter away from her. Ruby is still trying to keep up her show, but I'm watching the commotion now. She's shouting with her ex. Such drama. Now she's trying to walk away, but her ex grabs the nearest drink out of someone's hand and throws it on her. Is this really happening?

Then everything calms down and Deanna comes back and sits next to me, soaking wet, but still smiling. She turns to us, "Women, right?"

What is that supposed to mean? Brenda and Luis are laughing, so they must understand. I don't get it, shouldn't she be mad?

She whispers to me, "It's all good, pussycat. Enjoy the show."

I'm confused.

The show ends and everyone applauds. Except me, of course. I'm too full now. The waiter leaves one bill at our table, and Brenda says to me, "You got it, right?"

Luis says, "She shouldn't have to pay, this is her birthday celebration."

"No, it's okay. She's got it, babe."

Deanna pats me on the back, "Thanks, doll. You're awesome."

Ugh. Of course. Why would I expect anything different? I don't feel like fighting this one. I pull out my bank card and hand it over to the waiter with the bill.

Half of the crowd clears out while I'm waiting for my card and receipt to come back. Deanna goes to the bathroom, then her ex approaches me.

She gets close to my face and says, "You got a problem with me, bitch?"

"What?"

"Don't act like you don't know."

"Again, what?"

She pushes me and I almost fall out of my chair so I stand up to face her. Brenda and Luis stand up behind me.

I say, "I don't know what you're talking about."

"Yeah. Right." She shoves me.

"Who the hell do you think you are? You don't lay hands on me!" I shove her back. She grabs a hold of my hair and yanks it. I scream and grab her hair.

Then Deanna runs over and gets in between us, "Ladies! Ladies! Please."

We stop, both disheveled and breathing hard.

My opponent says to me, "You can have her." And storms back to her friends and they all leave Pinky's.

I turn to Deanna, "What the hell was that?"

"Oh, you know. Hey, listen, thanks for stickin' up for me."

"What? I was sticking up for myself because that crazy person came at me!" I'm not going to lie though, I kind of enjoyed getting some aggression out, and no one was injured, except maybe her ego since I won the fight.

Deanna continues, "I just didn't want to seem like a loser. I'll make it up to you. Anything you want."

CHAPTER TWENTY

A Neutral Place

On the ride home Deanna tries to explain. I guess I understand why she let her ex believe we were a couple, and I guess I saw it coming too. She did ask—but I said no.

She seems genuinely sorry and keeps pestering me about what she can do for me. I like revenge nowadays so I tell her to catch me an alligator. With any luck, she'll be eaten and won't bother me anymore. I'm smiling at the thought.

We arrive back at the house at sunset and while Brenda and Luis go inside, I walk with Deanna down toward the water. Limpkins are crying, but I don't know where any of them are or if one is Limpy.

I stand with my hands on my hips, "Well, go on."

She walks closer to the water, "I'm only doing this because you're such a good friend. I wouldn't do it for anyone else because it's so dangerous," then crouches down.

How crazy is she to consider me a good friend. I haven't done anything for her. She used me and now she feels guilty. She deserves whatever bites her.

"You hear that?"

"No." But I hope it's a gator.

She carefully walks along the water, getting further away. Then her arms shoot down into some tall grass, she shouts, and now is running back toward me with something in her hands.

She opens her hands to reveal an egg.

"That's not what I asked for."

"Sure it is. There's a wittle baby gator in here, and it was vewy, vewy dangerous to get it! The mom could be lurking anywhere. And I mean anywhere."

"Well don't bring that thing to me, go put it back or something." I don't even believe her anyway. It was probably a bird egg.

Deanna runs and puts the egg back. I leave while her back is turned, go back up to the house and sit on the porch. This did turn out to be an eventful birthday, not that I wanted to celebrate or anything. I stare out at the setting sun. Will Limpy ever come back?

Soon we're all sitting on the porch together. Deanna holds out something that looks like a cigarette, but I know it's not. She says, "Anyone want to join me?"

We're all staring at her.

She continues, "It's just a little Mary-Jane. Helped me through a lot of tough times."

Luis waves his hands, "Oh, no. None for me, thanks."

Brenda says, "I heard marijuana is a gateway drug, so no thanks."

I pipe in, "Don't act like you've never smoked pot"

"I haven't!"

"Back when we were young?"

"I was there but I never smoked any of it like you did."

"And it wasn't a gateway drug for me."

Deanna says, "This is the anti-gateway drug. God put it here on earth. There's actually been a lot of evidence to support the healing benefits of marijuana. If anything, prescription pills are more addictive and are the ones that'll do more harm if you're not careful. "

I nod.

She holds the joint out to me.

I'm undecided. I let a moment pass, then say, "Maybe some other time."

"Right on. Well, you guys mind if I go ahead?"

I say, "Have at it," then zone back out on the sunset.

Everyone is chatting away now and I'm trying to picture the blurry starry sky from last night. I think I could just use some more solitude. Why do these people want to be around me? I'm not any fun. I guess they're having fun despite me, like I'm some piggy bank figurine.

Brenda pokes me in the shoulder, "What do you think?"

"About what?"

"Cookout next weekend, here."

"Why here?"

"Well, Luis and I are going to spend time together

this week to get to know each other better. Then we thought it would be nice if I could meet the kids in a neutral place, and they've met you before. We'll keep it small, just me, you, Deanna, Luis and his kids. "

So I'm being used. Again. There's lots of neutral places. Every place but his house is neutral! I moved here for peace and I thought I finally found it last night, but now I'm bombarded by people in a caring disguise who want to use my house and my birthday as an excuse to do something.

"Please?"

"Or what? Your going to threaten me again?"

"No. Luis helped me understand that's not a healthy way to encourage you, and that it might be detrimental to our relationship."

"Got that right."

Deanna pipes in, "You wouldn't have to do anything. We are all going to pitch in. I think it's great to have a part in two people finding love."

I turn to her, "Why are you even still here? The only reason we met is because I was in the wrong place at the wrong time and you tried to hit on me."

"Hey, can't blame a gal for tryin'. Besides, I like your company."

"Why?"

"Your easy to talk to. I feel like I can be myself around you."

I can't think of a comeback for that. Actually, it sounded sincere, though I can't understand why she would feel that way. I bet it's because people like to be around those who are worse off so they feel better about themselves.

She continues, "You probably think I'm crazy,

latching on to you guys like this, but truth is, it's hard to find nice friends. I guess because I have so many walls up."

Luis says, "Would you like to talk about it? Why you have walls up? All of us have a story."

Great. Now I'm in some therapy session again. I appreciate Luis getting Brenda to back off me about moving in and being so annoying, but this is just not my thing. I don't need therapy, I need solitude, though I am kind of curious as to why she acts the way she does.

She takes a sip of her wine, then says, "Okay, so, hi everyone, my name is Deanna and I'm an alcoholic." She laughs.

A giggle pops out of me, but I quickly quiet myself.

"I understand your need to make jokes," says Luis, "it's a natural deflection when we are feeling exposed. But, it's okay, there's no judgement here."

Her face relaxes, "All right… So, when I was four, my mother gave me up for adoption."

Brenda says, "I'm sorry."

"No, it's okay, it was better I guess. She couldn't stop using and, in what I assume was a lucid moment, she realized she couldn't care for me. I can remember sleeping on the floor, always feeling hungry and getting yelled at for being hungry. So, it was for the best, and I didn't have to wait long to get a lovely couple to take me in. They had two daughters already, a little older than me, and they were nice enough. They didn't really understand though. So, anyway, long story short, my new mom and dad died in a car accident when I was sixteen. Their girls were eighteen and twenty, and neither wanted to take care of me. We were all in the car, but only us kids survived. I think they blamed me, so there I was, alone again."

Luis starts to speak but Deanna stops him, "It gets worse, of course. If that wasn't bad enough, I sought out my birth mother like an idiot. They found her and said she'd gotten clean. Man, I was so excited. But, when I met her, she said she only came to say she wants nothing to do with me, that I reminded her of her past life and she was getting her new life ironed out. So, I bounced around in a couple different homes over the next year until I had to just live on the streets." She sighs.

"So what did you do next?" asks Brenda.

"What I had to, to survive. I didn't do drugs or anything too terrible, but I've done some things I'd rather not think about. It's all in the past. Now I live life as it comes, trying to enjoy every day, and hopefully I'll find someone I can love, who will love me back."

Luis says, "That's an amazing story. I'm so sorry you had to endure all of those things, especially through your youth. All we can do is put one foot in front of the other, keeping our eyes looking forward, and keep hope alive in our hearts. Love will come for you, I'm sure of it. Thank you so much for sharing."

"I'll cheers to that." She holds her glass up.

Oh, what the hell, I clink my glass against hers, then Brenda's and Luis'. Reflecting on my own childhood, I see how fortunate I was in comparison. I hope I made Annie happy for the short life she had.

There's a somber silence broken only by Limpkins crying in the distance, and toads and crickets who have started their evening songs.

Deanna turns to me, "You know, it's obvious there's a special spark between your sister and Luis, and I think it would be a nice thing for you to do to give them a chance at happiness."

Why is their happiness put on me? They can go anywhere to introduce her to his kids. Why are they making it like I'm in the way? I'm not. They can do what they want. I guess it's because I'm older than Brenda, so she's looking to me for approval since our parents aren't alive anymore.

"Okay, fine."

Brenda jumps up, "Oh, thank you so much. This means the world to me."

Luis says, "I really appreciate your kindness, May. Truly. "

Deanna says, "Group hug!"

I'm practically lifted to my feet by everyone in their excitement and they all huddle around me.

"Okay, that's enough. I'm going to bed." I squeeze free.

The three of them walk inside with me and put their glasses in the kitchen, then head out toward their cars. I peek from the window to make sure they leave. Deanna drives off right away, but Brenda and Luis are making out by his van. Gross, I don't want to see that.

A few minutes later, I'm sitting on the futon and my sister walks in.

"What are you doing?" I ask.

She says, "I'm saying here."

Ugh. I get into my pajamas, then curl up in bed and look at my family picture.

She comes in with something in her hands and sits on the bed next to me, "I almost forgot," she sets a small framed picture on the night table, "I thought you might like a new picture to stare at."

It's another family photo of me, Dave and Annie,

but Brenda's in it too.

CHAPTER TWENTY-ONE

There's Two

I wake to the sound of Brenda laughing. Sometimes her voice travels like she swallowed a blow-horn. This is one of those times. The smell of coffee hits my nose. Well, I might as well get a cup. I shuffle out to the living room and freeze at the sight of her talking on her cell phone, oblivious to my presence. Something about her looks different. Maybe it's the way the sun is shining on her through the window, or a new hair-do? I can't put my finger on it.

She sees me, smiles and waves, so I scowl at her and continue shuffling into the kitchen. I pour my coffee then hold the mug in both hands, bring it up to my nose and take a deep breath in as I listen to her talking.

Something about food, weather, cookout —wait, the cookout is today? It's been a week already? Then I hear her say, "I love you too." She must be talking to Luis. How can they possibly know if they love each other, they haven't even known each other that long. Sounds like desperation to me.

Rounding the corner, she says, "Morning, sunshine," then stands next to me, "I'm so excited for today, thank you so much. Feels a little like old times right? But now *you're* the go-between."

I squint.

"Don't you remember? Well, I'm not surprised you don't, you were so love drunk and I was just the silly little sister."

"Brenda, what the hell are you talking about?"

"You know! How you and Dave got together, because of me? You really forgot?"

"Spit it out already." It hurts to think about him and I so long ago, we were so happy and young, and he was still alive. Who would have known this is how we'd end up?

"Well, I saw him riding his bike back and forth in front of our house, so I ran and told him you liked him. You were so mad when you learned what I'd done. But then I told you how he said he liked you too and that he wanted you to come out front. You didn't believe me, of course, so I think you went to prove me wrong. But there he was and he had picked one of mom's roses to give you and—"

"Enough. I don't want to hear anymore." I remember now. Vividly. It was the beginning of summer and the sun was warm but the breeze was still crisp. I was wearing my woven sweatshirt mom made me, and he was dressed in a long-sleeved, striped shirt and blue jeans. He had the cutest butt. I can still picture him perfectly, standing there in front of his blue bike, holding out the red rose to me. I knew instantly that I didn't just like him, I loved him... A tear escapes my eye and I wipe it away so Brenda doesn't see.

She wraps one arm around my shoulders, "It's an important part of the healing process to remember and focus on the good times."

"Stop throwing Luis' therapy mumbo jumbo at me."

"My point is: be happy for me. I always was for you when you found love and had a family. Plus, you might not ever have gone steady with Dave unless I was there. For years I never had what you had, and never thought I would. Now, because of you, I met Luis, and I believe this is my turn."

Yeah, while I rot away as an old widow.

"See if you can find it in your heart, that's all. If you do nothing else I will still thank you because I never would have met him without you and your crazy idea to up and move to Florida."

She should thank herself. She's the reason I'm down here. Besides, their little fling probably won't even last long. He has kids to consider, he can't jump right into a serious relationship. They're being foolish and those kids are the ones who are going to get hurt.

"Anyway, everyone will be here in a couple hours. You've got clean clothes in the dryer, and I also brought you some of your clothes from up north."

Ha! Probably winter clothes. Idiot.

Brenda leaves in her car. I don't care where she's gone. Now that I have some quiet time, I sit on the porch in my pajamas and drink my coffee.

A Limpkin cries and it's loud, from only a few feet away. I set my coffee down, then creep over to the railing that faces the marsh. "Limpy! Where have you been, you silly bird?" He's sitting in the grass below.

He cocks his head to look up at me.

"What are you doing down there?"

"Keow." He flies up into the oak tree.

Guess he doesn't want my company. Whatever. I take the opportunity to get a closer look at what he might have been doing down there. Is he living there? Right under my nose this whole time? There's a round pile of twigs and moss, with five blotchy brown eggs. They remind me of the egg Deanna said was an alligator egg. I knew she was lying.

"Krrr-eeeow! Keow! Keow!" He flies at my head then lands on the porch railing above the nest.

"It's okay. I won't hurt them."

"Keow!" He flaps his wings and lunges at me.

What the hell has gotten into him? I stumble backwards and bump into a rocking chair. He knows me, so why is he attacking me? Taking a second to watch and see if he's going to keep coming after me, I think about what I might have done to make him so angry at me. I guess because I was near his nest. But it's right up against my house. He can't be angry at me, it's my property! Stupid bird. I knew I never liked them. I don't know why I thought Limpy was different.

I cool my nerves with a quick shower, then rummage through Brenda's suitcase to get my mind off him. I thought for sure she brought clothes unsuitable for Florida, but actually she brought my favorite shorts and my most comfortable t-shirt. About time she did something right.

She's not back yet, and no one else has shown up, so I sneak across the porch and peek down to see if Limpy is still there. He is and— Wait, there's two down there! Which one is he?

I watch them longer than I should, but I'm just so enthralled. They're so tender with each other, the way they put their heads close, then inspect their eggs. It's sweet. I understand now, he was being protective. Or, it wasn't him at all, but his mate. That's probably it, she doesn't know me. If I was a bird, I would attack me too.

"Limpy?"

One of the birds, that's a little bigger than the other, looks up at me.

"Tell your girlfriend I'm not a threat." Or is she his wife? I don't know how that works.

The smaller one looks up at me, then flares out her wings.

I'm not giving her a name unless she quits being so aggressive. I know, I'll go find a snail to give them, maybe I'll find two. That ought to do the trick. I've come to enjoy my porch and if we are going to share my property, I'd rather not be yelled at and attacked every time I want to sit out here.

I toss two snails near them, then make my way up the steps and over to the railing above them. They've already cleaned out both shells.

"See, I'm no threat," I say to them.

"Keow. Keow."

"You're welcome." Part of me is glad I'm not his mate anymore, but part of me isn't. Who am I going to talk to now? "Limpy, can I talk to you guys?"

"Keow."

"So, there's a few people coming over today, and one of them is my sister, Brenda. You met her. She's the one that chased you away after you finally came inside."

"Krrr-eeeow!"

"Yeah. I know. I yelled at her about it. But my problem is, she really likes Luis. He apparently feels the same way about her, though I don't know why, and things are moving so fast with them. I just don't think it's a good idea when he has three young daughters."

"Krrr."

"Yeah, I guess Brenda's going to do what she's going to do no matter what I say."

"Keow."

"But that doesn't mean I have to be happy for her."

CHAPTER TWENTY-TWO

Where Is This Going?

Brenda's back so apparently it's time for the stupid cookout. She has a skip in her step as she carries five bags in each hand. For someone with no money, she sure did buy a lot of stuff. Enough hot dogs and hamburgers to feed the town, plus the buns and all the usual fixings and condiments. Part of me wants to say something sarcastic, but I'll let it go.

She squeals, "I'm so excited I just can't stand it!"

Well, if you can't stand it, then stop.

"If his kids are half as sweet as he is, then I'm definitely in love! Oh, I meant to ask you, have you noticed anything about him that would be like a red flag? Anything I should worry about?"

"Well…"

"Oh, no. What is it? —Wait, don't tell me, I don't want to know… Aah! Okay tell me."

I stare at her.

She takes a few deep breaths then composes herself.

I say, "I was only going to say that I can't think of anything. He was always nice I guess."

"You guess? What does that mean?"

"Ugh, nothing. Don't read between the lines."

"Well, tell me how you guys met. He's told me his side, but I want to hear yours since he's so modest I'm sure he left some parts out."

"They're going to be here soon."

"Okay, well quickly then."

Damn it. "His cologne is a bit strong, but he opened my car door for me, so that was nice. Um, he set me up in the motel because this place was bare, then took me shopping… Let's see, he remembered me at Thanksgiving, Christmas and my birthday, but that might have been because I bought him that van."

"Shut up! You bought him that van? And you yell at me about handing you a grocery bill?"

"If you could have seen what he was driving his kids around in… Anyway, that would be my caution: he's broke."

"I don't care about how much money he has."

Right, because she's going to milk it from me. The settlement money has to last me until I die or I don't know what I'd do. She can fund her own life.

"So, he's a good guy?"

Who can say who's good or bad? I nod and shrug.

"Do you approve?"

Well, they do seem well suited. "Yeah, sure."

"Thanks big sis. I really appreciate it."

I still don't understand why she cares if I approve or not.

A little while later Luis pulls up. He unloads a small grill out of the back of his van. His three daughters get out and loiter close to him. Aw, they're wearing flowery sundresses. How cute. Annie had one similar when she was young.

Brenda bursts out the door to help him. I watch them from the window. She gives each one of them a hug, but the girls are a little unsure. Then Luis starts rolling the grill to the shade under the oak tree, but a little too close to Limpy.

I run out, "Not over there!"

All three of his daughters yell, "May!" at the same time, run over to me and give me a hug.

"Yeah, hi girls, tell your daddy to move that thing away from my birds."

The oldest asks, "What birds?"

"Just tell him to keep it closer to the tree so it's away from the house." I point and the girls run off.

Brenda walks up to me, "It's amazing how kids flock to you. You're a natural mom."

That hurts. I'm not a mom anymore… I go back inside to watch from the window.

Deanna pulls up, gets out of the car, and I can hear her from here shouting, "I got booze! Let's get this party started!" She brings a few bags in, goes back twice for more. It's a lot more than booze. Unloading onto the dining table, there's two bags of chips, potato salad, coleslaw, a fruit bowl and two pies, along with a couple different types of soda, lots of beer and two bottles of wine.

That beer looks good. I haven't had one since before Dave died and there's something about having a beer at a cookout that seems so right. Shit. I don't have a bottle opener. I'm holding the beer and looking around.

She must have noticed. "Here, let me get that for you." She takes my bottle and twists the cap off.

"Oh." I take a swig then go sit on the porch.

I'm soon joined by everyone.

Luis says, "The grill is all set up and ready for meat, but first I want to introduce my kids." He ushers them to stand in front of him, "This is Isabella, my oldest, she just turned nine. Sofia is six, and Zoe is four."

He then says to his daughters, "You remember May, and that's Deanna and Brenda is the extra special lady friend of mine that I was telling you about."

Brenda says, "I'm so very happy to meet you girls." She kneels down and hugs them, all three fitting in her arms.

When the hug is over there's an awkward silence, but Deanna's good at breaking those. She says, "Are you girls hungry? I know I am! Who wants to carry the hot dogs?"

The girls all say, "I do, I do!" and follow her inside.

Luis kisses Brenda on the cheek and whispers something, probably that everything is okay, because she seems a little worried the girls won't like her.

Then everyone goes over to the grill and they are all chatting and laughing while getting it started, and the girls are helping put the hot dogs and hamburgers on it.

Deanna yells to me, "Okay if I put on some music?"

I nod.

She goes to her car and brings out an old portable radio then finds a station playing songs from when I was a kid. They're called classics now, of course. It's nice listening to these songs that I haven't heard in so many years, but at the same time it makes me feel old.

Annie would've loved her because she always gravitated to the people who were considered weird. We were alike in that way and now that I think about it, Deanna's growing on me.

I bet Dave would have enjoyed having a male friend like Luis. Toward the end of his life he didn't have a good friend because he was working so much to provide for me and our daughter. He thought it would be worth it at the time to secure our retirement, but we didn't save much.

Luis says something to his youngest daughter, Zoe, then she runs up on the porch and stands in front of me. We look at each other for a moment without saying a word, though she's smiling. I work up a smile in return, then she pushes a chair close to me and sits in it.

I ask, "What did your daddy say?"

"What?"

"Never mind." Must not have been important.

"I have a bird too. He's blue."

"That's nice."

"Can I see your birds?"

"No."

She scrunches her face for a minute, then says, "Why not?"

Hm. I can't think of a good reason. She's soft spoken and not hyper like my Annie was at her age. I guess it'll be okay. "You have to be quiet."

Zoe nods excitedly.

We stand up and I lead her over to the side railing of the porch and point down.

"Where?"

I point again. She's trying to fit her head through the spindles. I lean over to make sure the birds are there, then pick Zoe up around her waist with her back to me so she can hold onto the railing and look down.

She whispers, "Oh! So cute! What are their names?"

"Well, one of them I call Limpy, but the other one only showed up today, so she doesn't have a name yet."

"Limpy?"

"Yeah, not very creative. They're Limpkin birds, so, you know."

"Oh…what about Birdy?"

"No, Limpy."

"For the other one."

Birdy? Really? And I thought Limpy was bad. "What's the name of your bird?"

"Bluey."

"Oh, you know what? I think Birdy is a good name." Besides, I can call her something else when everyone leaves. I lower Zoe back to the ground to stand on her own.

"Ready for fixins!" Deanna jogs up the steps then goes inside.

I tell Zoe, "Go help."

She wraps her arms around me, "I wanna stay with you."

Ugh. "All right." We go inside together.

Deanna's washing and chopping the lettuce and tomato, and laying it out on a platter I didn't know I had. I pull the sliced cheese from the fridge and hand it to Zoe,

"Go take this to your daddy so he can put it on the burgers."

Zoe runs out the door with the cheese. Guess she didn't want to stay with me that badly. I watch her as she carefully navigates her way down the steps, runs over to her family, that apparently includes Brenda, who picks her up to put the cheese on the burgers. That's sweet, and would make a cute picture too.

I sit at the dining table while Deanna is finishing the prep for the burger fixings. Now she's putting the buns, condiments, coleslaw and potato salad on the table in front of me.

Soon everyone is inside and picking whether they want a burger or a hot dog and plopping spoonfuls of the coleslaw and potato salad on their plates. I pick a burger *and* a hot dog, because why not? Then I fill my plate with a little bit of everything.

Everyone has a seat. Seven people, seven chairs. I thought it was a strange number for a dining table, but maybe it's meant to be? I can't even remember the last time I sat around a full table for a meal. It's kind of nice, but sad too—for me anyway. I'm always the sad one I guess.

When everyone is done, the dessert is served by Brenda who cuts both pies to give everyone an equal piece while dishing every last bit of it out. There's laughter, cut by the occasional squeal from a kid because another one is picking something off their plate or something. Reminds me of one of Annie's birthday parties when she was younger.

Luis asks his daughters to join him outside for a moment. Then, when they come back in, the girls are all giggly and he walks over to Brenda and holds her hand while standing next to her. "So, while everyone is here, there's something I want to say." He takes a deep breath, "When I first saw you, I knew there was something special about you. After my wife passed, I didn't know if I would ever find love again, but I had hope." He turns to me, "Because of you, May, I found love."

I smile, but I'm not sure if I mean it. Where is this going?

He turns back to Brenda, "I know you feel the same way. This past week has been amazing—you are amazing. I explained everything to my daughters and they want me to be happy, and there's no time like the present, so…" He kneels while still holding her hand.

She covers her mouth with her free hand.

Damn it. What is he doing? He can't be that stupid! They hardly know each other! She literally just met the kids!

He continues, "Will you do me the honor of marrying me?"

She squeals, "Yes! Oh, Luis, yes! I love you, I love you so much!" She leans in and kisses him.

Zoe hands him a small box.

"This ring belonged to my grandmother, I hope you like it." He opens the box to reveal the ruby and diamond ring he gave me for assurance while fixing up this place. He slides it on her finger and it fits perfectly.

"I love it!" She kisses him again.

He stands up and they embrace each other as if they were magnets and actually meant to be together. I'm in shock. Deanna pushes up on my chin and laughs. I guess my mouth was gaping.

CHAPTER TWENTY-THREE

A Trained Professional

The cookout is coming to an end and Brenda hasn't stopped smiling. Neither has Luis for that matter. I guess I'm happy for them, but it makes me sick to look at them. I had that once. Maybe I'm supposed to be content with having had it at all, but it sure has left a hole in my heart and I wouldn't wish this sadness on anyone. She would be better off learning from my misery and staying alone.

The kids are playing in the shade between the grill and the porch. Then all at once they stop and scream. They're pointing toward the side of the house. Oh no, my birds! I run down and head toward Limpy's nest.

The kids are screaming, "No! Don't go there!"

I don't listen. When I near the corner of the house I'm confronted by a huge freaking alligator. I dig my heels in to stop and fall backward onto the ground. "Get away from my birds!" I take off one of my sandals and throw it. One of my birds flies away, but I don't know which one, and I can't tell if the other is still sitting on the nest or not.

As I stand up I'm joined by Zoe who is crying hysterically. I nudge her to go away, but she has latched onto me. The gator hisses and takes a couple steps toward us. We must look like a good snack. He's distracted from my birds and their eggs, but I'm not about to feed him Zoe.

Deanna screams, "Don't run! He's faster than you, I guarantee it. Just stay there for a second." Then she walks up and stands in front of us so we can sneak away.

We all watch her from the porch. Her arms are spread out, side to side, and she's moving in a crouched position while keeping the giant reptile's focus on her. She says, "Someone get me a long stick."

Luis runs off toward the woods on the other side of the house and returns with a branch that's about four feet long and about an inch thick. He hands it over to Deanna from the porch. She doesn't take her eyes off the gator, so he touches the stick to her hand and she grabs it.

I sneak over close to the railing and peek down. One of my birds is still sitting on the nest. "Fly away, dummy!" It doesn't budge. I step back and feel Zoe wrap her little arms around me. I hold her and we watch.

Deanna says, "Somebody get my phone and call the number listed as "Alligators". Tell them to bring a truck and that we've got a big one for the farm."

Brenda runs inside and a minute later returns. "They can be here in half an hour."

"All right."

Isabella says, "What's going to happen to him?"

"Well, he's not afraid of people, so it would be dangerous to let him stay here. I know some folks that will take him to live out his life on an alligator farm where people can enjoy his size. He'll have a nice life and nobody will get hurt."

The beast lunges up, mouth open, fangs glistening. She moves to the side of it, keeping her crouched stance. Then she taps the stick on the gator's side. It whips its body to where it's head and tail meet. She jumps to avoid the tail, then works her way around and taps his other side.

She continues doing this and starts talking to us like we're an audience and she's putting on a show. "What I'm doing now is tiring him out. He doesn't have as much energy as the little fellas, who are actually more dangerous. We're lucky he's a behemoth." She keeps working him and working him.

The kids are enthralled now that the danger has somewhat passed. The gator's lunges are not as strong and his movements are slower.

Deanna asks, "Anybody got any duct tape and a towel?"

Brenda shrieks, "Don't tell me you're going to try and catch that thing!"

Luis says, "I don't think that's a good idea. There's got to be some kind of professional we can call."

Keeping up with her performance, Deanna says, "You're looking at one. Didn't I tell you? I moonlight as an alligator trapper."

She's full of surprises, and she's proving to be quit handy.

She continues, "So…Duct tape? Towel? Anyone?"

"Yeah I might have them." Luis runs to his van and rummages, then jogs over to her but stops abruptly a few feet away. "Um, how do I—Where do—"

She says, "Just hold on to it and stay right here. You want to jump the tail? We want to get him blindfolded and taped up so he doesn't run off."

"I—I don't know if I can," Luis says. Then he looks up to the rest of us on the porch. Brenda nods to him, then he says, "I will do my best. My fiancee is watching."

"It's okay, This is how everyone starts. I'm going to jump on his back and what I need you to do is then jump on his tail. When you get on him, be prepared that he's stronger than you think, even though he's tired. So you're going to jump on, but keep your knees on the ground and squeeze them together so you can hold with your hands too"

I just can't believe my eyes that she knows what she's doing and that the cookout turned into a proposal and now alligator wrestling. Maybe I'm dreaming.

Deanna says to Luis, "Ok. You ready? Jump on his tail, right after me." Then she tosses the stick away and leaps onto his back with her hands pressing his mouth closed against the ground.

Luis drops the tape and towel then jumps on the gator's tail. He's dragged back and forth a little bit while he gets his grip.

"Scooch up closer to me so he doesn't whip you, and stretch your feet back while still on your knees to hold his tail in place. You're doing great."

He does as she says and that seems to hold better.

"Where's the tape and towel?"

"Oops. It's over there."

"May? Brenda? One of you want to hand them to me?"

My sister is looking at me like I should do it. I'm looking at her like she should do it. She's clearly terrified though and says, "C'mon, you know those things freak me out!" Like they don't scare the crap out of me too?

Ugh, whatever, they've already got him under control. I stomp down the steps, grab the tape and the towel, then slowly approach Deanna at the head of the beast.

She reaches her hands under the jaw, then lifts the whole head up so it can't open its mouth. "Would you like to do the honors?"

"Are you freaking kidding me? The honors?"

"You kind of have to. Just do it. Start the tape, then wrap it around and around right here, between his nostrils and his eyes so we can keep his jaw closed. You need to go around several times, then when you think it's enough, do a couple more."

This reminds me of when I tasered Brenda, and I've never touched such a huge reptile before, so I'm actually having a pretty good time. I tape up the mouth, paying close attention to my every move and every little twitch of the enormous jaws.

The gator's head jerks to the side and Deanna screams as if her hand has been severed.

I'm so startled I shriek and fall backwards, kicking the ground to push myself away from the beast who I think has gotten free and is going to eat me now.

But, Deanna is laughing hysterically.

"Not funny!" I dust myself off.

"I couldn't resist." She lowers its head back down to the ground. "Okay, no more jokes. This is serious business. Put the towel over his head, and tape above and below his eyes so he can't see and we don't hurt him."

The creature becomes extra still when I place the towel over its head. Deanna and Luis are dripping in sweat, but Luis is struggling a bit more. He's doing a good job though. I doubted he'd even do it at all. Hell, I didn't expect to be participating either.

Finally a truck pulls down the driveway then backs up close to the gator and two men jump out. They take over handling the gator.

Deanna hollers to Brenda and the kids, "You guys wanna touch him before we load him?"

Brenda apprehensively brings the excited kids over who waste no time in gently running their little fingers down the creature's scaly back.

Luis tells his fiancée, "C'mon, babe, if I can jump on him, you can touch it. It's safe now, I promise." He guides her closer and helps support her. She looks like a child herself. I understand, I felt the exhilaration too.

Then we all back away and the kids huddle with me and Brenda, as Luis, Deanna and the trapper men lift the gator's upper body into the back of the truck and heave the rest of him up. Success. Annie would have loved this experience.

The trappers drive off, so we all head inside for some water. They're all praising each other on jobs well done. Then Brenda says to Deanna, "You are amazing, you know that?"

"Aw shucks." Deanna says like it was nothing, though she's blushing.

Luis says, "You really are! You saved us all. Who knows what would have happened if you weren't here."

Now she's loving the attention, offering tips and

tricks and answering all their questions. I sneak away and sit on the futon.

A while later it seems they've noticed my absence and I'm approached by Brenda who says, "So, I want to ask you something."

"Now what?"

"It would mean so much to get married…here."

Ugh.

"That sounds like a wonderful idea!" Luis says, "This is the first place we met, after all. If it's okay with you, May."

How come I can't find a happy medium with these people? They either desert me or are suffocating me. I suppose it could be worse, they could be asking for money, and I know they can't afford to rent a venue. Damn it. I can't think of a way to say no. Besides, if it's here, they I don't have to go anywhere and I can watch from the window. "Yeah, okay. Fine."

Deanna says, "Ooh! I'm ordained, so I can totally marry you guys. I mean, if you want."

There's another money saver. They are lucking out. Maybe they are meant to be?

The couple look at each other, then in unison say, "We'd love that."

"Sweet! I'm stoked. When do you guys want to do it?"

Brenda says to Luis, "What about July first?"

"Your birthday? I love it! That gives us about a month to plan and decorate, and for you to get your dress and everything, however you want to do it. Yeah, I think we can make it work!"

"I want to keep it simple. I have an idea in mind for decorations, but that depends on what May is okay with." She turns to me, "Since you are the reason we met, I thought it would be nice to decorate with flowers everywhere. In honor of you, May Flower."

It's fine. I nod.

Luis says, "My brother in-law does landscaping, I bet he could help us out with that." He turns to Brenda, "Would that be okay? I don't have much in the way of family of my own, but I'm still close with all my in-laws. I hope that's not a problem."

"No problem at all, I just hope they like me too."

She hasn't met the in-laws? What the hell did they do all week? Never mind, I don't want to know. "I assume you want to stay here until then, huh?"

She says, "Actually, I'm going to stay with Luis, except for the night before the ceremony."

"Fine."

"I'll stay if you want," says Deanna.

"Um…Nah, I'm okay."

"Suit yourself. But if you change your mind, I'd be happy to."

I nod and sip my beer.

Luis turns to Brenda, "You ready to go home?"

She giggles and nods.

Deanna says to me, "I should go too, unless you want me to stick around for a bit? Make sure no more alligators come up?"

"That's okay. I'm going to get some sleep."

She hands me another business card, "Well, call me if you need me."

CHAPTER TWENTY-FOUR

Not a Goddess

When the dust settles after everyone leaving, I let out a sigh then lay on the living room floor. Anyone else would probably have a smile on their face while reflecting about all that's happened, but my cheeks are drooping into jowls.

How can I be happy for them when they're being so careless? How can they not see that this is going to end in disaster? What if something happens to Luis? Then Brenda, who's never raised a child, will be stuck with three kids that aren't even hers? I doubt she's considered anything like that. I bet that alligator was a sign. Why else would it show up the day he proposes?

Limpy and Birdy are inspecting their nest. I drag

a rocking chair closer to the side of the porch. "You're welcome. You almost got eaten today, stupid."

They don't even look at me.

"You two need to be more careful now that you have little ones."

They gently touch beaks.

"Yeah, well you couldn't fight off that gator with your love, so I doubt it conquers all. By the way, how long did you date before you became a family?"

Limpy stretches out his wings.

"That fast?"

Birdy situates herself on top of the eggs in the nest, then sits down.

"I guess it's possible. I knew right away with Dave, but we were teenagers. Brenda and Luis are adults and there's kids involved. How would you have felt—Birdy, I'm talking to you." I snap my fingers and she looks up at me. "How would you have felt if Limpy already had little ones running around?"

She shakes her head.

"Yeah, his kids should have a mother figure, but what if she's a terrible mother? They'll end up being my responsibility and I am having a hard enough time being me right now."

Limpy flies away.

"Guess he doesn't care for girl-talk."

Birdy's tidying the nest around herself.

"Anyway, if I think about it, what were the chances that I would meet Luis in the airport on the day he was swapping out the brochures, and that he would stop by on the same day Brenda comes to town? Nah, it's coincidence. He probably swapped out those brochures every other day for all I know, and they both came to see me for my birthday, not some random day. Birdy, what do you think?"

She's silent.

"Limpy does all the talking in your family, huh? At least you're nothing like my sister. She always has something to say. I wonder if Luis' kids even like her, or if they realize they don't really have a say in the matter. Poor things. I feel bad for them, having her thrust into their lives as a new mommy without even knowing her."

Limpy returns to Birdy with a snail in his mouth. He sets it down, digs his beak into the shell, then feeds it to her.

"Yeah, I agree. It's always better to have support when it comes to kids. I had a hard time when it was just me and Annie. But even if Dave hadn't died, if he maybe had an affair and left me or something, I still wouldn't bring some new guy into the family."

Limpy finishes tidying the nest for Birdy.

"I see what you mean. If it's the right person, it makes life easier. Maybe Annie would have had a better life if instead of comforting me when I had a crying fit, she was able to laugh with me more. Maybe I would have been happier with a new love interest around. But Dave did die. I was sad. She was sad."

"Krrr," he coos.

"Yeah, but we had good times too, though it was usually when Brenda came over to lighten the mood. She was always better at making Annie laugh than I was."

He flies up toward me and lands on the porch railing. "Krrr."

"I'll try." I guess I owe it to her to try and be happy for them. She was supportive when I lost my husband. It's just that she became so annoying after Annie passed.

Always around, yammering on and on when I wanted to be left alone.

It's going to be so hard for Luis' kids. Only a few years before Isabella is a teenager. Then there's Sofia, the middle child. Poor, unpredictable middle child. I've heard some horror stories. Even though she's sweet enough now, who knows how she'll end up? And Zoe. Little naive Zoe. If she likes me so much, what does that say for her common sense? Eh, it's a crap shoot for all of them, especially with Brenda as the stand-in mommy. I'd say their situation is like a Jack-In-The-Box toy, only nobody knows if it's Jack in there or some hideous monster and only time will tell.

As the sun starts to set, I'm suddenly afraid for my birds. What if another alligator comes? Only one of them flew away earlier, so one of them would surely die defending their eggs. I should have had Deanna put up a fence or something. Would a fence even stop a gator? Well, I've got my flare gun, but what if I hit Limpy? Shit, what can I do?

I picture myself coming out here tomorrow morning to find feathers everywhere, the nest destroyed, the eggs gone and a gator swallowing the last of my bird-friend. No. I cannot let that happen. I'm just going to sit here and keep watch for them, after I get a beer and put Deanna's phone number by the corded wall phone in the kitchen. Yep, I'm going to stay awake and keep watch. Then I can figure something out tomorrow in the daylight.

As the night gets darker and the moon rises, sounds become more clear. I hear Limpkins for sure, crickets, something I can't identify, frogs or toads or both — what is that? There's rustling in the bushes. Is it another alligator? A snake? Some wild hounds preparing to attack me? I shiver as I finish my beer, then scan the dark tree line that's swaying in the wind, moonlight glinting off the leaves.

A bright flash of lightning in the sky is quickly followed with a crack of thunder. I jump and scream. The electricity in the air has my hair standing on ends. My heart is racing.

An owl hoots, then some weird chirping, not like a bird, like I don't even know what. Is that a howl? I run inside, grab another beer, the flare gun and a big flashlight that Deanna must have left me. I should call her. No, I'm being silly. Grow up, May.

Returning to the porch with a strengthened resolve, I plant myself in the rocking chair, beer in one hand, flare gun in the other and the flashlight on the floor by my side. I pretend I'm some sort of cowgirl outlaw that nobody messes with. In my best country accent, I yell, "You come messin' 'round these parts, I got somethin' for ya!" I wave the gun in the air. "That's right, y'all stay out there where you belong!" I take a swig of my beer.

Thunder cracks open the sky and rain pours down. Did *I* just make that happen? Oh, the possibilities with that kind of power! I bet I could even bring Dave and Annie back to life. I'd be a goddess. We would sit on golden thrones with a mass of people laying gifts at our feet. We could make all the alligators toothless and cuddly, all the birds would be able to show expressions on their faces, and no one would die, ever.

Gah! Something's touching my shin! I fumble over the chair, kicking the flashlight, flinging my beer down to the other end of the porch, and the flare gun goes flying out into the bushes on the other side of the nest.

"It's nothing. It's nothing. Pull yourself together, May. Come on." I take a few deep breaths then retrieve my beer. Luckily it didn't all spill out.

I start down the steps, then feel the rain. The flare gun is probably ruined now. I find the flashlight then sit back down in my chair. A moment later I feel something on my leg again. This time I look first. It's a little stupid moth.

Great, some goddess I am, scared by a little bug. I peek at my birds but it's only Birdy. She's not getting too wet, but it doesn't look comfortable either. So, things get tough and Limpy's nowhere to be found? Typical man, right?… Actually, my Dave wasn't like that and Luis doesn't seem like that either. Why is that even a saying? I don't think there's a 'typical' type of any person.

I scoot my chair closer to the door, then try to get comfortable. At least the thunder isn't that loud anymore, just rumbles in the sky. But now I can hear all the lurking animals and critters better. I sip my beer.

Aw, Limpy has returned. I guess I was wrong about him. I'm probably wrong about a lot and don't even know it. I mean, you don't know what you don't know, right?

The rain slows to monotonous dripping drops, weighing my eyelids down. I'm going to rest my head against the back of the chair and close my eyes, only for a minute to refresh.

CHAPTER TWENTY-FIVE

Just Stay Here

"Keow! Keow! Keow!" Limpy screams.

My eyes dart open. "What! What is it?" The rain has completely stopped now and the part of the porch that was wet earlier has dried. I must have fallen asleep.

"Keow!"

I lean over the railing. Birdy is sitting on the nest and Limpy is facing off with another Limpkin, they both have their wings flared out.

"Stop it! No fighting!" I take my flip flop off and throw it at the intruding bird. I miss. I reach for my other flip flop and remember I already threw that one at the alligator earlier. I've been walking around in one flip flop? Why don't I notice these things?

The intruding bird flies away. At least that's all it was. I can't believe I fell asleep. "C'mon, May, wake up!" I slap myself in the face.

An animal squeals over by my car. What the hell is that? It sounds so horrible, like something being squeezed to death or something. I grab the flashlight and shine it out by my car, then scan over to the trees. What. The. Hell. Is. That? I stare at it. It moves a little and the squealing stops. Oh hell! It's a freaking huge, disgusting snake! I hate snakes! I run inside and call Deanna.

"Pick up. Pick up."

"Hello?" She sounds like she just woke up.

"Deanna!"

"Yes, mommy?"

"No! It's May. Come over, now!"

"Huh? Oh," she clears her throat, "What's happened?"

"It's a s-s-snake!" I almost can't say the word.

"Be right there." She hangs up.

I stay inside, pressed against the dining window, shining the flashlight out onto the creature devouring some poor unsuspecting critter. They're ruthless! I don't want to watch this, but I can't risk it getting out of my sight, then who knows where it'll end up? Probably in the freaking house somewhere. I shiver.

Two minutes later, Deanna pulls up and jumps out of the car. I run out onto the porch and shine the shaky light back on the snake, then scream, "Watch out! It's right there!"

"All right, calm down," She comes up next to me so she can see from my point of view. She's dressed in a jacket over a white t-shirt, boxer shorts and unlaced construction boots.

"In case you're wondering, I didn't have time to put pants on, so don't judge me."

"Just get the snake!"

She laughs, "Okay, keep doing what you're doing. Keep the light on it. Lets see, yep, you got yourself a boa constrictor and by the size, looks like a female. Males are smaller."

"I don't care what kind it is, get it away from me! I hate those things."

"Aw, hate's a strong word. All she's doing is surviving the only way she knows how. I mean, she's not even bothering you really."

"It *is* bothering me. It's on my property."

"Well, honey, you live on Florida marshland, what did you expect? Maybe I could teach you a few things to make you feel more comfortable here."

"Will you please get that thing away from me?" I can't even think about anything else, let alone learning about the vile creatures.

She goes back to her car, pulls out two long rods, one with a loop on the end, the other with a hook, and a tall cage type box. She puts the loop around it's head and tightens it, then slides the hook under the mass of it's body bulging from dinner, picks it up and lowers it into the box. Easy. Once the lid is shut and locked, she loads it into the backseat then turns the car on.

"Where are you going?" I yell.

She rolls down the window a crack, then turns the car off. "Just givin' her some air." She joins me on the porch. "It's easier when they've eaten. Slows 'em down."

I gag.

"Now do you want me to stay?"

"Well, duh!" I go and peek down through the

railing to check on my birds. They're fine, but I'm going to have to keep a closer eye on them. Deanna and I can take turns. Wait— "How did you get here so fast?" What if she was one of the noises in the bushes?

"I happened to be nearby."

I cock my head. "Really? In the middle of the night? In your pajamas?"

"Yep, and actually it's almost four, so technically it's the middle of the morning. Totally acceptable."

"Whatever. Watch my birds while I make some coffee."

I bring out two cups of coffee, then slide the other rocking chair close to her. She sips her coffee and it's quiet for a minute. I'm enjoying this silent company. It's kind of funny, now that I think of it, how I want a bird to talk to me but not people.

Then she breaks the silence, "Ok. I have a confession to make. I didn't just happen to be nearby..."

"Yeah, I figured that. You lurking in my bushes?"

"No, after I left yesterday I had to run a couple errands, then I got tired on they way back to town. I was passing right by your place again so I kinda parked by your mailbox to sleep."

"That's odd." I'm not sure if I believe her. Why would someone choose to sleep in their car when their house might be a short drive away? Maybe she was being extra cautious, but it's still weird. Something doesn't feel right about it. Maybe she's like a functioning lunatic with wildlife skills. Oh hell, what if she snuck down here, left the snake, then ran back to her car? Would she do that?

Deanna has her head bowed down. Is she crying? That's the last thing I need. I've already got all the Limpkins doing that, and sometimes me too.

I ask, "Do you do that often?"

"No, that was the first time at your mailbox. Worked out in your favor though."

True. And she's not crying, but her eyes are a little red like maybe she was going to. I know that look. I've held back enough tears to fill a lake. "How often do you sleep in your car? I mean, are you crazy or do you just like it?" Oops. I didn't mean to say that last part out loud.

She laughs, "Well, I don't think I'm crazy, but if I was, how would I know, right?"

I squint. That's true too. She makes a lot of good points, probably smarter than me and that's why she comes off as a little eccentric. Or maybe she's a genius serial killer! "You didn't by chance plant that snake there to make me call you…did you?"

"Seriously?" She giggles, "Don't flatter yourself. Coincidences do happen, but I call it divine intervention."

Hm. "Fine, just checking."

She continues, "Anyway, I've been sleeping in my car for about a month now."

"Why?" How does a grown woman get to be homeless?

"Shit snowballed and next thing I know I don't have enough money in the bank to stay where I was, or enough to get another place. Why spend that money on motel rooms that are about as clean as my car?"

"Running water, that's why. Where do you shower?"

"Oh, I know the guy who runs the gym in town. He lets me use the shower there."

"Sounds like you know a lot of people. No one has taken you in?"

She shakes her head.

Hm. "So, why don't you have any money? You're single right?"

"Yeah, and you're awfully chatty tonight, you know that? I think I like you better as a listener, pussycat."

"Don't call me that." Though I guess I deserved it, I am being pretty nosey. It's so weird how someone could get to her age, my age, and not have any money. She doesn't even have kids or anything. Although I would be pretty close to her situation if I didn't get that settlement money. I can't picture me sleeping in my car though, other than that first night here, but that was because of that other alligator.

What would I do if I didn't have that money? I shiver. I'd be living with Brenda. But at least I would have her. Judging by Deanna's childhood, she doesn't have anyone.

"Yeah, it sucks, but I'll be okay. I always bounce back somehow."

"But don't you do like a thousand different jobs? What kind of money are you paying out?"

"Well, the wildlife stuff is volunteer work. It's something I love doing and it keeps me sane. The EMT thing is unpaid too, I just like to help people. I once had a lady almost choke to death right in front of me, so I decided to learn how to save lives. I don't get paid for being ordained, walking the dogs at the shelter or playing with the cats in the shelter. I do still get paid to do some gator wrestling from time to time. Besides that, I'm currently between prospects."

"Okay, then what was your previous paying job?"

"Oh, I've worked lots of different jobs, but nothing I'm as passionate about as helping people and wildlife. They'd always get upset when I ran out on work to help someone. People need to get some perspective, for real. I love saving lives, it makes me feel like I'm here for a reason."

That makes sense. I get it. Something about the sky catches my attention, though there's nothing spectacular about it. Maybe Annie wants me to help her? This same feeling came over me when I had the opportunity to help Luis. It must be my family. Why else would Deanna choose to sleep at *my* mailbox on the night a big snake decides to eat its dinner in my front yard?

I say, "Just stay here for a while if you want."

"No, I couldn't impose on you like that. Luis told me about your grieving and everything. By the way, I'm so sorry about your husband and daughter."

I knew it. It is a sign. Okay, Dave and Annie, you got it. "You're staying here. The futon is pretty comfortable. It's not much, but it's a roof, running water and poor company."

"What about the bedroom?"

"What? No, you can't sleep in my bedroom. What is wrong with you? I'm not a lesbian!"

She laughs, "I mean the guest bedroom, since Brenda's staying with her fiancé."

"Oh, right. Yeah, sounds good."

CHAPTER TWENTY-SIX

Mediation

The sun is shining and Deanna's leaving to go drop that snake off somewhere other than here. I didn't bother asking where. As luck would have it, as soon as she's gone, Brenda pulls up.

"Was that Deanna I just saw leaving?"

"Yeah? People can have gay friends without being gay, you know!"

"First, that's not what I meant. Second, what's with the attitude? And third, I was only asking to see if you decided to let her stay here until she can get back on her feet?"

Bleh, she sounds like a mother already, but the annoying kind that lists things off one-two-three. I did that once with Annie and I felt so uptight I never did it again. Wait, "How do you know?"

"She told us, when she was telling us about her childhood."

I admit to zoning out, but I would have caught that part. She must be lying.

"Anyway, wanna go dress shopping with me?"

"No."

"Really, May, you didn't even think about it."

I guess that was a little harsh, but I don't want to get roped into paying for the dress. I can't be her personal bank, she needs to figure things out for herself.

"It would mean the world to me. And I'm not expecting you to pay either. I'm looking for something simple like a sundress. Although, if you *did* want to gift it to me, as a wedding present, I wouldn't say no." She winks.

I don't want to. I didn't get any sleep last night and I probably won't get any sleep today either because I have to keep an eye out on my birds so nothing eats them. Hm… I have an idea, but I'm not going to like it. "If you watch my birds for a couple hours so I can get some sleep, then I'll go shopping with you."

"Okay, deal!"

"But they have to still be alive when I wake up, or I'll kill you."

"Got it. No problem."

"Sit over there, and don't bother them."

"Sheesh, I can watch a couple of birds."

I have my doubts, but sleep is calling me. I belly flop on the bed.

When I wake up, it's still daylight. I was hoping to sleep through the day to get out of dress shopping, but my body apparently has other plans. When I emerge from my bedroom, Brenda's inside and Deanna's back. They're chatting in the dining room.

"Brenda! What about my birds!?" I stomp my foot.

"Relax. I can see them from here."

I run over and put my face next to hers to see if she really can. Yeah, okay, fine.

Deanna says, "I was just dishing the low-down on the best place to get a dress. She invited me to go with you guys. You okay with that?"

"What? Oh, fine." I need more sleep, but since I'm up I could use some coffee.

Brenda says, "Made you some coffee."

Okay, this is getting creepy. It's like she's reading my mind. She did that earlier when I was thinking she would want me to buy her dress.

"How do you—"

"How do I know what you're going to say?"

Spooky.

"Uh, hello! Because we're sisters and after Dave passed I basically took care of you and Annie. Then I had to take extra care of you after Annie passed."

Hm. I admit she helped after Dave, but when I became alone she was more like a fly, always buzzing around no matter what I did.

It's quiet for a few minutes, then Deanna says, "So, do you mind if I go with you? I mean, I don't want to intrude if you want it to be a sister thing."

I snap, "Sure, why not, I guess I'll be expected to buy lunch too?"

Brenda says, "May! That's rude. No one is asking you to pay for anything."

"Right. It's *expected*. Like I said."

Another awkward silence.

Then Deanna says to me, "Maybe I shouldn't stay here, if you feel like I'm going to be looking for hand-outs from you."

"It's not you, it's her," I point. "She's always on me about money. I won't be pressured into buying useless crap."

Brenda says, "So my wedding dress is useless crap?"

"Yeah. I think so."

Deanna says, "I'm going to go outside, let you two hash things out." She shuts the front door behind her.

Brenda continues, "This dress is going to be the most beautiful thing in my life, no matter what it costs. Know why? Because I'm getting married in it! A good sister would want to be a part of that."

"Well, I'm not a good sister."

"You used to be."

"Just go do your own shopping and stop trying to get money out of me. Live your own life for once!"

"I'm about to! I'm in my forties and about to have my own family for the first time ever. Why can't you want to be a part of my happiness? I was always there for yours."

"Yeah, I know, whether I liked it or not."

"Why are you being like this?"

"Because you're so freaking annoying!"

Deanna comes back inside, "Hey, I can hear you guys and I think I know what the issue is here. Do you mind if I...?"

I say in my most sarcastic tone, "Sure! Please shine some light on this disaster."

Brenda says, "Yes. Your opinion is welcome."

"Great. So, May," she looks at me, "You're hurting, so it's easy to confuse someone's help with being a nuisance. What you've been through is horrible, but you have to recognize that your sister has sacrificed years of her life to help you through it."

I fold my arms.

She continues, "And Brenda. Sometimes maybe you do need to give May some space. She's a big girl and can take care of herself."

"No, she can't."

"You have to let her try."

"But she fell face-first into a glass table! She could have killed herself. I was scared that maybe she was trying to and I couldn't bear to lose my sister."

I flail my arms in the air, "I fell on that table by accident because you were annoying me!"

Deanna says to me, "But did you hear what she said? She was afraid that you might try to actually kill yourself, and it's understandable to worry about that, given your circumstances."

"I wouldn't kill myself. If God wants to take me, then so be it, but until then I'm just trying to mind my own damn business."

Deanna says to Brenda, "There's your answer, so you don't have to worry about that anymore." Then she turns to me, "What are your other concerns?"

"She wants to milk the settlement money from me."

"What settlement money?"

Brenda answers, "For the wrongful death of her daughter. She got paid like a million bucks. She's got plenty now, but before the check came in, her savings had run out and I had to pitch in out of my pocket to support her, even though I was grieving too. Is it so bad that I would like her to do the same for me now that I'm in need?"

I say to Brenda, "What did you ever pay for, huh? You had access to all my money. That's why I'm broke without the settlement, because you kept spending it!" Shit, that's right. I never took her off my bank account. She's probably withdrawn half of it already, but then why is she complaining about being broke?

"I've never touched your money, except to pay your bills—*your bills.*"

"You're so annoying. You expect a return for something I don't even know you freaking did!"

Deanna says, "So, it sounds like maybe you do owe your sister a little."

I plant my fists on my hips. "If she's even telling the truth. The first thing out of her mouth when she saw the check was 'lets go shopping.'"

Brenda says, "It was your birthday!"

"Whatever."

"All right, calm down," says Deanna, "So, Brenda helped take care of you and your daughter, and the money is from your daughter in a way. Would Annie want her to have any of it?"

If it were up to my baby girl, she'd probably split it. But she was a child.

Brenda shoves her phone in my face, "This is your bank account. Do you see any purchases that aren't yours?"

I try to scroll down on the screen but I pushed a button or something and the screen changed.

"See? Thats why I do these things for you. Because

you can't." She pulls up my account again and slowly scrolls down for me. And she's right, there's only my stuff.

I say, "Not everyone knows how to use a cell phone."

Deanna giggles, "Girl, we need to bring you into the times here."

Yeah, I probably could make more of an effort to learn technology. Annie used to try and teach me, but I'm a terrible learner when it comes to that stuff.

Anyway, focus. I say to Brenda, "So you've had access to all the money, this whole time and you didn't spend any of it?"

"Right. So you can quit thinking of me as the bad guy. Besides, if that's what's driving a wedge between us, then I don't want any. Me, Luis and the kids, we have each other, so we will be fine no matter what." She takes a deep breath, "Damn it, May, you know what my problem is? You should be happy for me! Why can't you do that for me?"

"Because *I'm* not happy! Don't you get it? I'm a freaking burden!" Through my anger, a tear streams down my cheek. I've never said that out loud before, never even thought it really. But I know, deep down, it's true.

"You're not a burden…"

"I am."

Brenda hugs me, then Deanna wraps her arms around both of us.

This is the first time a hug has felt good, but it's squeezing my thoughts into my memories of Dave and Annie and the pain. I mumble, "My family is dead."

Deanna says, "Not your whole family."

She's right, and now I feel like shit for saying that

when she is truly all alone in the world. Any kind of family she has wants nothing to do with her. What an asshole I am to be upset that my sister is around me too often. "I'm a horrible person."

Brenda runs her fingers through my hair, "Don't say that, you know that's not true."

"I am being horrible though." I pull away from the hug and turn to Deanna, "Of course you can stay here as long as you need. You've been a good friend."

"And I'm handy too! But seriously, thank you, I appreciate it."

I turn to my sister, "Thank you for everything you've done for me. Annie and I will buy your dress and even pay for the flowers and anything else you need for your wedding. It's *our* gift to you."

"Only if you want to because I—"

"Damn it, Brenda!"

We all stare at each other, then burst into laughter. Some things may never change, but if we can laugh about it, then I guess we'll be okay. Maybe she's not the one who changed. Maybe I've become crotchety and impatient. Probably.

I look at Deanna, "Who's going to watch my birds while we're gone?"

"Oh, they'll be safe during the day."

"But that gator came in the afternoon."

"Yeah, but that's unusual, and he was probably attracted to the noise of the cookout, lookin' for scraps. Your birds will be fine."

I nod then turn to Brenda, "So, you want a sundress huh?"

CHAPTER TWENTY-SEVEN

Killjoy

In a local clothing shop, Brenda's twirling around in yet another sundress and I'm starting to wonder if she's doing it just for fun now. She's tried all the pastel colors and even a few loud patterns. This one is brown, but it's so dark it looks black. I mean, come on, seriously?

I'm going to regret this: "Are you sure you don't want an actual wedding dress?"

"Of course!" She spins to face me, "But, wouldn't it look silly since we're getting married in your yard? Plus it would be expensive."

"So? I'm paying now, remember?"

"What do you think, Deanna?"

"I don't think it's silly if that's what you want. I

mean, you'll probably stare at the thing hanging in your closet for the rest of your life, so why not get something fancy?"

"You're absolutely right! Lets do it!"

Luckily, this town has everything and a bridal boutique is a couple blocks down. It's small, but packed with plenty of options. Too many.

An hour later Brenda has tried on half the dresses in this place. Deanna and I are browsing while she's changing again. I reach for a dress and she's reaching for the same one. Dear God, let this be *the one*.

I knock on the fitting room door. Brenda squeals and snatches the dress, then moments later she bursts out, looking radiant. Deanna whistles the way a construction worker would at an attractive passerby. My jaw is gaping. She looks stunning. The halter top and jeweled waist accentuates her physique perfectly, and the layers flowing down to the floor are as soft to the eye as puffy white clouds. It doesn't even need to be tailored.

"What do you think?"

"You look so beautiful." And I'm not just saying it to be done.

Deanna says, "Wow. I liked the dress on the rack but, damn girl. Work it!"

Brenda giggles. "So, this is it. We've found my wed —" Her giggles turn to sobs, "I'm sorry, I'm so happy." She shuts herself in the fitting room for several minutes then comes out in her regular clothes holding the dress gently in her arms, her eyes red from crying.

Best one thousand, thirty-one dollars I've ever spent, and the amount is also Annie's birthday. My baby girl had a hand in this, I'm sure of it.

We tuck the dress safely in my closet at the house,

then head back to town for lunch at Pinky's.

Sitting at the bar, Brenda pulls out a piece of paper and hands it to me. It's a doodle of my yard with everything mapped out for the ceremony, including a walkway from the porch steps ending at an arbor by the old oak tree, with urns sitting on either side. She drew question marks above each urn, so I guess she still has some flower decisions to make. Looks nice. I hand it over to Deanna.

She says, "Oh, yeah. We could definitely make this work. Lighted topiaries would look great in those urns."

"Ooh, yes!"

"We could probably get a lot of the stuff today. I know a guy at the garden store who could probably hook us up with a discount. Hang on, I'll call him." She steps away from us.

Brenda says to me, "Thank you again. I love that you're a part of this with me."

"Yeah, well, what choice do I have?"

"Is that how you feel?"

"I'm kidding." Kind of. "But really, you could stay engaged for a year before sealing the deal."

"What's the point of waiting when everything is so perfect?"

"Because relationships are always great in the beginning when everything is new, but marriage can be hard work."

"I know that, but this is true love."

"Everyone says that. Have you even met the in-laws?"

"Some of them, but I have a few weeks to meet the rest. They seem nice."

"And that's supposed to be enough time for them

to accept you playing mommy to the kids?"

Brenda rubs her temples. "Don't ruin this for me. Please."

"I'm being realistic, there's a lot you two aren't considering. You're only what, forty-two? You've got plenty of time to ease into the situation."

"No one knows how much time they have. You of all people should understand that."

"Of course I do! That's my point. What if something happens to Luis and you're stuck with his kids? Or the in-laws take them from you after years of bonding? Or something happens to you and that family has to go through heartbreak all over again? It's selfish."

"May, you should hear yourself."

I slap my hand on the bar, "And you should listen to me for once in your life!"

Deanna returns, "Girls! No fighting."

There wouldn't be a fight if Brenda would use her brain. I ask Deanna, "Don't you think they're moving too fast? I mean, buying the dress is fine, but everything else feels rushed for no reason."

"Well, let me put it this way: I've known a few couples who eloped after a couple days, some worked out and some were annulled. Then I've known people who waited years only to get divorced six months later. It depends on the people. Believe me, I've thought about this plenty. If I ever found a spark like I see in them, I wouldn't wait."

"You're supposed to be on my side!"

"Sorry pussycat, I don't take sides and I don't stand in the way of love."

"I'm being realistic!"

"And a killjoy."

Brenda nods.

"Fine, I'll keep my mouth shut, but if the day comes when it all falls to shit, I get to say, 'I told you so.'"

She says, "Deal," and we shake hands.

Deanna puts her hand on ours, "What would you two do without me?"

"Yeah, yeah." I say. Then our food arrives, so I add, "Shut up and eat."

She giggles.

Brenda asks, "So, what did your friend say?"

"Oh, right. We're good to go."

"Yay! Let me text Luis to see if he and his brother-in-law can meet us there."

We finish eating then drive around the block behind the grocery store. Who would have known a small town would have such a huge garden store. They've got everything from flowers to trees, pots to waterfalls, pavers to arbors.

Brenda says to me, "What do you think about daisies, marigolds and jasmine?"

"Do what you want, it's your day."

"Yeah, but you have to live with it after."

"They're flowers. Have you seen my yard? Anything will be an improvement."

Deanna is talking to the guy she knows while Brenda and I look at the arbors and urns which are set up by the pavers and other stone-work decorations. Maybe I ought to have pavers laid in the front yard? Then it wouldn't be so dirty all the time since the grass apparently doesn't want to grow there.

Brenda says, "You should put pavers in your front yard! I mean, if they aren't too expensive."

How does she do that?

"Did I read your mind again?" She wiggles her fingers in my face.

"No. But now that you mention it, that would look nice. I miss having some pavement around the house like up north."

"Since you brought it up, what are you going to do with that house? I'm staying down here now, so you could move back if you want."

I sigh, "I don't know. There's so many memories up there. I've got half a mind to box everything up and sell the house. But at the same time I'm sweating just thinking about doing it."

"Then let it sit for now. I locked everything up and your neighbor Carmichael is watching over it for you."

"Seriously? Mister 'my dog died so I know how you feel'? That neighbor?"

"Did he say that?"

"Yeah."

"Well, I guess he was trying to be nice. People don't always know what to say."

I try to put myself in his shoes, walking up to my door and talking to me for the first time since the news of Annie spread…Yeah, I see her point.

"Anyway, he's got our numbers if anything—shoot, that reminds me, I totally forgot I brought your cell phone down for you! Not that you got any calls from anyone, besides me before I realized you left it behind."

"I don't need it."

"You might."

"Okay, I don't want it."

"Well, I'll put it in your nightstand in case you want to look through the pictures."

I don't know if I want to do that either.

Then Deanna walks over, "All right, so here's the deal. He can get us ten percent off, but if we do a large enough order, he'll do fifteen."

Then Luis walks up and kisses Brenda on the cheek.

She asks, "Where's your brother in-law?"

He shakes his head, "I'm sorry, baby, he's swamped with work right now."

Yeah right, that's an excuse.

He continues, "But I cleared my day so I can help."

She hugs him, but I can see it on her face she knows I'm right about the in-laws disapproving. No one says anything though, and I agreed to keep my mouth shut, so we move on.

Hours later, we've all decided on a simple, rounded arbor, two concrete urns so tall they come up to my waist, two spiral, lighted topiary plants to go in them and four carts worth of flowers. Deanna helped me pick out some wood and chickenwire for her to build a fence around my bird's nest too. The best part? Everything is being delivered!

At the checkout, I arrange to have pavers professionally laid for part of the driveway then expanding out to most of the yard in front of the house, including a walkway to the oak tree. I picked the natural stones that are all different shapes and sizes so it doesn't look too modern with the old cracker house, but are still sturdy enough to park cars on. The guy who's going to measure will come with the delivery of everything today, then the pavers should be installed within the week.

I didn't get that sick feeling from the purchase either and I almost didn't even think about it. A part of me was glad to be shopping today, though if anyone asked, I'd deny it.

Back at the house, Brenda and I are directing the delivery men on where to put everything. Luis and Deanna build the fence around Limpy and Birdy's nest, with plenty of clearance so they don't feel threatened, and low enough that I can step over it, I think.

A couple hours later the delivery men are driving away in their truck, the fence is done, Brenda and Luis seem to be in deep conversation under the oak tree, and Deanna and I are each enjoying a beer, sitting in the rocking chairs on the porch to watch the sunset. Turns out she can be quiet company.

Now the couple is coming this way, walking hand in hand. I assume whatever they were talking about had a somewhat positive resolution, but Brenda's face is still furrowed with anxiety.

She says, "We're going to take off. Thank you guys for everything today."

Deanna holds up her beer, "Our pleasure."

I blurt out, "Everything will be fine." I didn't even think about it. Must be my old self peeking out.

"Thanks sis. I love you."

"You too."

They drive off and Deanna and I sit in silence.

Then she says, "So, tell me about Dave and Annie, if you don't mind. I've told you my story, but all I know about yours is their names."

Gosh, where do I even start?

"What was your daughter like?"

I picture Annie's beautiful smile and the way she would crinkle her nose before she laughed. "Annie Jewel Johnson…" I pat my hand against my chest, "My beautiful baby girl was perfect. She was so creative, always doing art. Not the usual art kids do though, not my girl. She liked to do productions and make sculptures out of anything she could get her hands on. I remember she made me this cereal necklace for my birthday once, and I was happy with it even though it wasn't up to her creative level. But then she yanked it away from me, threw it on the ground and started singing, 'You are worth more than that to me!'" My voice cracks trying to sing it out. "Then she pulled out a sculpture of a three-dimensional heart made out of nuts and bolts that she'd glued together and mounted on a small piece of wood. She had spray painted it gold."

"That's so sweet…"

I nod.

"How old was she?"

"She was fifteen when she died. A stupid zip line accident at camp."

"Oh, I'm so sorry."

"Yeah."

"Was Dave a good husband?"

"He really was. Better than I deserved, I'm sure."

"What did he do for work?"

"Furniture sales."

"Was he any good?"

I smile, "No. Not at all, but he tried and worked hard and never gave up. Wore a suit every day. Very dapper."

"So, how did he pass?"

"Heart attack. He was working a lot of overtime and I think the stress was too much. I should have gone back to work by then to help out, but I loved being home with Annie and he never said it was a problem."

"Well, you know it's not always stress that causes

heart attacks…sometimes it just happens."

That's a comforting thought. She would know too since she's got training for that kind of stuff. "We were high school sweethearts, you know. The day he proposed, the weather was—"

"Beautiful?"

"No, awful, actually. He'd planned a picnic by the lake and it was cold with that constant drizzling rain. I mean a thunderstorm would have at least been romantic, like you see in the movies, but it was awful. Neither of us cared at the time though, and we even still tried to eat our picnic. I had a feeling he was going to ask me something, but I thought he was going to ask me to move in with him, you know, get a place together, so I stuck through the terrible weather. We were both shivering and shaking and he said, 'If I can have a good time in this weather with you, we can get through anything. Will you be mine forever?' and held out this ring." I raise my left hand.

Why does she have that weird look on her face? Shit! Where is my ring? I stand up and look all around the ground. It must have fallen off somewhere. "I can't believe I lost it!" Then I remember, "Oh, that's right, I had to pawn it after Dave died. I'd gone back to work, but it wasn't enough to send Annie to camp…I guess I forgot to go back for it." I slump back into my chair with my head bowed.

"Damn. That's tough…No way to get it back?"

"It's been years, so I don't think so. Do you think there's a chance?"

Deanna shakes her head, "Probably not. I'm sorry."

I finish my beer.

"Let me get you another." She goes inside.

I'm such an idiot. I look at the cloudy night sky and apologize to my family. If I hadn't pawned the ring, I'd have it forever, and maybe Annie would still be alive.

"Here ya go." She hands me a beer.

I chug a good bit of it.

"How about your birds?"

"What? What about them?"

"Brenda tells me you don't like them, but then you wanted that fence for these two."

"Oh, I don't know. Limpy bonded with me, and it was kind of sweet."

"He bonded with you? Pussycat…did you mate with the bird? Are those *your* eggs down there?"

"What? No! He just fed me a snail."

"Ohh shit, you ate a snail!"

"I—No—I mean, I pretended to eat it because he offered it to me. It's part of the bonding process! It's in the book!"

We look at each other, then she starts laughing. I realize how it sounds now and I find myself laughing with her.

"You mated with a bird!"

I almost spit my beer out, "I—I did. Yes, I did."

"You ate a snail. For a bird."

"It was so gross. He dropped it on my chest. I had to pretend to eat it or I thought he was going to peck my eyes out!"

She's laughing so hard she can't form any words.

"I don't even like birds!" I snort.

"And then he found another chick?"

"Right? I didn't eat his snail good enough!" I'm laughing so hard now I can barely breathe.

"That's a riot!"

"Me, of all people!"

We laugh for a few minutes and it feels so good, I don't want it to end. But then the moment passes and silence creeps in as we drink our beers.

"You're a good friend."

"You too, pussycat—I know, I know, stop calling you that."

"Eh. It's growing on me."

"Do I get a nickname?"

I shrug.

"Are you ever gonna shave those legs?"

We laugh some more.

CHAPTER TWENTY-EIGHT

Maybe

Two weeks have passed uneventfully and living with Deanna has been more enjoyable than I thought it'd be. Brenda's only stopped by a couple times and nothing has tried to eat my birds. My pavers still haven't been installed though, so all the plants and flowers are still sitting in pots. Supposedly it was a 'typo' in their system, then they had to order more, but they will be coming out this week for sure. We'll see.

Deanna's making breakfast for the first time since she's been staying here and if it tastes anything like it smells, I'm in for a treat. I open the front door to go check on my birds.

She hollers, "They're fine." Then she peeks around

the corner, "How do you like your eggs?"

"Oh, I'm not sure anymore." I sit at the dining table with my back to the kitchen so I can look out the windows.

"I'll surprise you."

A few minutes later, she sets two plates in front of me. One has a sunny-side up egg, a small pile of scrambled eggs and a piece of toast. The other has pancakes. Mmm, I haven't had pancakes in forever. There's only two, stacked one on top of the other, but they're huge. She sets a bottle of pure maple syrup and two glasses of orange juice on the table, then sits down with two plates of food identical to mine.

This looks so good. Brenda's food would always be burned or soupy, which is another reason I'm not sure she'd be a good mother— Eh, that's a mean thought, lots of mom's can't cook. I wonder if Luis can?

"Well? You gonna try it or not?"

Oh, right. I start eating a little of each type of egg. I give her a thumbs up.

"So, which do you prefer?"

"Um, I don't know, I like them both."

Deanna laughs. "I'm the same way. Sometimes I'm in the mood for one or the other, sometimes both."

That makes me feel a little better. I had to put up with crappy cooking for so long, I guess I have to learn what I like again.

"You like the pancakes?"

They taste like how my Dave used to make them. "Very much." If I close my eyes, I can almost feel him here with me, Annie too. Saturday morning breakfast was a tradition, and no matter how broke we were, we at least had pancakes.

As we're cleaning up, Brenda walks in. "You guys! It's horrible."

Deanna says, "What happened?"

"We announced our engagement and wedding date to Luis' in-laws and," She starts to cry, "they don't approve. At all! They were shouting at him in Spanish, and pointing at me. I couldn't take it anymore, so I left and came here."

I fold my arms. "I tried to warn you. You can't expect everyone to be understanding."

She snaps, "I came here to get some support! Can you hold off on the 'I told you so' for five minutes?"

Whatever. I lay down on the futon.

Deanna sits Brenda down at the dining table and tells her, "Take a couple of deep breaths and let's talk about it. They probably don't understand, but you have the rest of your life with Luis to prove them wrong."

"Right? It's not like I'm pressuring him, he proposed to me! I even asked him last night if we should wait until my birthday next year, or pick a different date, and he refused."

"See? Then don't worry about the rest of them."

"But his kids are going to be flower girls and I wouldn't want the family to miss it."

"Look, they either come or they don't. This is your life."

"I just want to fit in to their big happy family, even though they're his late-wife's family."

"But they don't even know you yet. Give them some time."

"So I should put it off?"

"I'm saying they need time. And guess what? Time is time whether you're married or not, right?"

"Yeah."

"So, follow your heart. They'll come around either way, I'm sure." Deanna hugs her. "You know what you need?"

"What?"

There's a knock at the door. Brenda opens it and is embraced by Luis and his daughters. Deanna sits in the wicker chair next to me, then Zoe runs over and climbs onto the futon with me. She's a sweet little thing, so much like my Annie at that age. Isabella and Sofia follow and now I have to sit up so we can all fit. I don't know why these kids care to be around me.

Brenda pulls away from Luis and says, "I'm sorry I left like that. I thought it would be easier for you guys to hash things out as a family without me standing there. I hope you don't think I run away when things get tough, because I don't."

"No, no, no, *I'm* sorry you had to see that. I would have told them myself if I knew they'd react that way."

She bows her head.

"They're good people though. They just don't know you yet like I do."

"I feel like they hate me."

Luis gently lifts her chin, "No one could ever hate you."

"But, maybe we really should wait until next year."

"Is that what you want?"

"No, but I don't want to cause problems either."

"Well, I don't want to wait. I love you. They'll come around."

Deanna hollers, "That's what I said!"

They laugh, then he gets down on one knee, "Will you still marry me?"

Brenda starts crying again, "Of course!"

A few awkward minutes pass by with us all watching the love-birds gaze into each other's eyes, when Deanna goes over to them and says, "So, what I was saying earlier is: You know what you need? A bachelor and bachelorette party!"

Brenda squeals, "Yes!" She turns to Luis, "What do you think?"

He says, "Oh, you go ahead and have your fun. I don't think I'll do one."

Deanna says, "Why don't we merge them and all of us get away for the day and—and go to the casino!"

Brenda says, "I've never been. It sounds like fun, but I don't think we can afford it right now."

"Pfft. You don't need that much, it's about getting away for the day. Plus, I've gone before with twenty bucks and when that ran out I sat and watched people and still had a blast. You wouldn't believe the mix there, young people all dressed up like hookers and old people, a lot more old people than you'd expect."

"Have you ever won anything?"

"Nah, but even when I lose it's still cheaper than going to Disney, and almost as entertaining."

They laugh.

Luis says, "I think it's a great idea, something completely different from everyday life."

Brenda looks at me with pleading eyes and says, "Will you come?"

"Maybe."

"What if we went today? Like right now?"

"I'm kind of busy today." I've never been to a casino, and it does sound interesting. But I doubt it'll happen anyway. These two have too many issues to work out.

"Yeah? With what?"

Deanna says, "With nothing, that's what."

"I have to watch my birds!"

"I built them that fence. They're fine. Just the other day I saw a little gator try to get them, but he couldn't."

"What!? When?"

"You were sleeping."

"Well, did you get rid of it?"

"Nah."

"What if he comes back?"

"Oh no! What if another one comes, or another snake? Guess what, you live on the marsh. The fence is good, your birds will survive."

Hm. Oddly enough, I like the sarcasm and I believe her more because of it. "Fine."

Luis says, "Let me see if my sister-in-law will watch the kids. She probably will, she's supportive."

While he's on the phone, Brenda takes the opportunity to quietly ask me, "Will you consider helping us have fun?"

What is that supposed to mean? Oh, she means money. Hm. Lets see if that's what Annie wants me to do. I wait for a sign, looking around all the corners of the room and out the windows. Nothing catches my eye.

Then, Luis, putting his phone in his pocket and pulling out his keys, says, "We have a green light! I'm going to drop off the kids, then I'll come back and pick everyone up! Sound good?"

Brenda says, "Sounds perfect!"

Deanna gives a thumbs up.

I shrug.

CHAPTER TWENTY-NINE

Happy Kitty

Deanna and I both take a shower in our respective bathrooms. I swear I can hear Brenda in the living room giggling through the noise of the running water. She must really be excited.

When I come out, dressed in my purple track suit, I see them putting some snacks in a bag. How long a drive is this? What have I gotten myself into?

Then Luis pulls up in his van and honks the horn.

Brenda runs out, Deanna follows and I trail behind. I refuse to run. So, naturally I'm the last one in the van, and sitting in the back again, though I guess I don't mind so much now. It makes sense for the couple to be up front together.

During the drive, I pay more attention to my sister and her interaction with Luis. If I don't think about my own situation, then yes, I think I can be happy for them because they seem to genuinely care for each other. I'm also glad they packed snacks. I bet Brenda talked to him about his cologne too, because the van doesn't smell like he spilled a whole bottle in here.

An hour later we arrive at the casino. Good thing I decided to wear my track suit because it's chilly in here. It's still nothing compared to the cold up north though, which I don't miss at all. It's loud here too, bells and whistles and music everywhere. It's like sensory overload.

Deanna says, "Who wants a drink?" and she heads toward the bar.

I might as well, but I'm going to be keeping an eye on how many Luis has. Not that I think he would overdue it, but I'm not taking any chances. I'll gladly join my family in Heaven, but I'd rather not die in a gruesome car accident.

Sipping on my wine, I follow Brenda, Luis and Deanna who are all beaming with excitement. I'm not quite at their level. It's interesting, but nothing to go jumping around about. There are, however, some very interesting looking people milling around.

We stop at a row of four machines that are all different from each other. Luis sits at Lucky Panda, Brenda sits at Fairy Riches, Deanna sits next to me at a machine called Gold Goddesses and I get stuck with Happy Kitty.

"Look, pussycat!" says Deanna, "A machine made specially for you!" She laughs.

It is kind of funny. I raise my glass and take a sip. Then I look down the row and watch as each of them pull out a single dollar bill to insert. Maybe that's just what you do here? I look at my machine. Each credit is two cents, but each try costs forty credits. That's eighty cents, so they each get one try out of their dollar bills? Seems a little ridiculous then to only put in one dollar at a time.

I hear Brenda's machine singing and she says, "I won a dollar!"

Great, so she gets one more try. This is dumb.

Luis is pulling out another dollar bill to feed into his machine.

Deanna says to me, "Give it a whirl, pussycat!"

I take another sip of my wine, then set it down on the little space between the machines. Opening my wallet, I realize I don't have any cash.

Deanna must have seen into my wallet too and says, "C'mon, I see an ATM over there."

I stand in front of the ATM while Deanna acts like my bodyguard. Then, when I insert my card, I feel a warmth come over me. I close my eyes. Annie? Dave? Is that you? Is this my sign that I'm supposed to help them? But this is throwing money away, and for what? Oh, right, it's a special occasion and I did say this was cheaper than some other entertainment. Well, the true test whether my family wants me to give them play money will be if I get that sick feeling.

I withdraw four hundred dollars, one hundred for each of us, and I wait. I only feel the warmth. Guess I'm supposed to give.

When I try to hand Deanna a hundred dollar bill, she says, "No, no, I couldn't. Give it to the happy couple, this is for them. You get your card back?"

Shit, I forgot about my card. I spin around, grab my card and receipt and shove them in my wallet. What an idiot. But then I try to hand over the hundred dollar bill again.

She says, "Hey, actually, you should go ahead and break that here for them, you know, into twenties or fives or something."

Good idea. Am I riding the stupid train tonight or something?

She helps me break the hundreds into five dollar bills. I don't think I've ever carried such a wad of cash before. We join Brenda and Luis who aren't even playing anymore. They're just enjoying each other's company, flirting and all that. Probably out of money already.

I lean in between them holding a wad of five dollar bills in each hand to them. Their faces light up.

Brenda says, "Oh, May! Thank you so much!"

Luis says, "No, I—I can't."

I walk away, "It's a gift. Have fun."

They giggle and start kissing each other so I turn around to Deanna and hold out her hundred dollar wad of fives, "Take it or I'm kicking you out of the house when we get back."

She laughs. "All right, all right. But I'm buying your drinks out of this."

"Fine."

Sitting at my Happy Kitty machine, I feed a five dollar bill into the slot. Before I press the button, I check to see what everyone else is doing. They're all focussed on their own machines. I could just sit here, pretending to play, and save my money. No one would even notice.

Deanna leans over to me, "I don't hear any bells going off over here. Here, lets turn your volume up." She taps a button on the screen a couple times and I hear a series of beeps that get louder and louder. Great.

I say, "Did you win anything?"

"Nah."

"Oh?" She spent the whole hundred dollars already?

"Relax, I only played five bucks. This machine's a dud, I can tell."

I don't know why I was upset, I gave it to her to do what she wants with it. Well, Annie gave it to her.

Then Deanna presses the button on *my* machine.

"Hey! What'd you do that for? Play your own game!"

She giggles.

My screen shows the same white kitten, almost in a row." Hm. Interesting. I think that would have been a big win. I think about hitting the button.

Then I hear Brenda holler, "Luis got free spins! He got free spins!"

"Sweet!" says Deanna, "How many?"

"Twenty!"

Wow. Guess we will be sitting here for a while. I lean toward them. I can't tell if he's winning anything. Okay, stupid kitty, lets play.

Deanna hits my button again. I smack her in the arm and almost spill my drink, but then I see I won five bucks. That's not a bad return. I think I understand now. People play these games for entertainment with a chance of leaving with more than they came with. It's probably rigged though, I bet no one even leaves with a smile.

She says to me, "Play, or I'll press it for you again."

I glare at her, but she smiles bigger at me. I never met someone who was immune to my glares. Well, she's not going to make me do something I'm not sure I want to do, so I put my hand over the button to shield it.

Then she presses my hand down and makes me push the button.

"Damn it, Dee!"

"Oh, pussycat, did you just give me a nick-name? How sweet."

"Shut up."

She laughs then points to my screen. "Whoa!"

It's one giant white kitten and now my machine is making bell and whistle sounds like crazy. The screen is flashing the words MAJOR JACKPOT and gold coins are flying all around the kitten.

Brenda and Luis are leaning way over in their chairs to see my screen, and Deanna is jumping up and down behind me.

I can't even believe my eyes. I'm frozen as the machine keeps counting the win: one hundred, two hundred, three hundred.

Brenda yells, "How much is it?"

Deanna answers for me, "We don't know yet, it's still counting!"

The machine finishes and the total is exactly one thousand thirty-one dollars. Annie's birthday. My baby girl is here with me. It has to be her and Dave. They're both here! I smile.

I print the ticket to take my money and winnings out of the machine, then we all head up to the cashier. I think I heard Luis say he won ten bucks from all his free spins, so I guess I did pretty good with the jackpot. Even though I have over a million dollars in the bank, this win still feels like a lot.

The cashier pays me, and I give Deanna, Brenda and Luis each three hundred dollars. They don't put up a fight about taking it either, probably because it's from the casino and not me personally.

CHAPTER THIRTY

Dreaming?

We stop for dinner at the restaurant inside the casino and each of us orders a steak dinner. I listen for a few minutes to their voices, not paying attention to what's being said, and it's still apparent they're all so happy. If three hundred dollars is enough to put a smile on their faces, why can't I feel good with over a million? Because my family is dead, that's why.

Our steaks arrive. I stab mine, cut off a piece, then shove it in my mouth. I'm sitting here chewing like the cow I'm eating and I don't know if I'll ever be truly happy again. As soon as I start feeling good about something, I'm reminded of my losses. Dave and Annie probably wouldn't want it to be that way, but when the thought pops into my head, what am I going to do? Tell it to get out? Ignore it?

Deanna bumps her shoulder against mine, "How's your steak?"

I shrug. Everything is tasteless.

She whispers in my ear, "You know, you're doing a wonderful thing for those two love-birds."

Then why do I feel like shit? I work up half a smile.

"You're a good person."

Am I?

We finish eating and are waiting for the bill, when a group of waiters bring a round cake, that's more like a giant cupcake, and has a single candle burning. They're singing a happy birthday song *to me*. Not the song everyone sings at home though, because that would be copyright infringement. No, they're singing some awkward, upbeat version it.

I say, "It's not my bir—."

I'm poked in my side and Deanna whispers, "Free cake."

Okay, I'll play along. Maybe it'll cheer me up. They tell me to make a wish so I close my eyes and wish for my family to be alive then blow out the candle. Everyone applauds. When I open my eyes I'm still sitting with Deanna, Brenda and Luis, all clapping and smiling at me. I twist and turn to look around the room, but no Dave and Annie. I guess my wish didn't come true.

The cake is enjoyable, but not spectacular like I hoped. I'm glad we didn't have to pay for it either based on the outrageous price of the steaks. We all chip in to pay the bill then head straight for the bar. I order another glass of wine.

Deanna leads the way around the casino and I watch them all play a few more machines, then I sit to play a one called Dragon Dollars. It eats my twenty bucks within minutes. That's enough for me with these machines. I already won. The allure is gone, if it was ever here at all.

After meandering around for a while, we find ourselves at a roulette table. I don't care to play, but they are all excited. How can they be so happy all the time? Especially Deanna, with all that she's been through, how did she find happiness? She's probably faking. That's what I need to figure out how to do. People don't get it. When you're sad, you don't always want company, but that's what they think is best for you. And, I don't know, maybe it is. Maybe I would have accidentally killed myself by now if I didn't have my sister always popping in on me.

There's nowhere to sit over here. Oh, perfect, there's another bar within eyesight of the table. As soon as I get comfortable, they spot me and start waving me over. I wave back at them.

Deanna runs over to me, "C'mon, you're going to be my lucky charm." She practically drags me back over to the roulette table and now I've got wine dripping down my hand. Good thing my outfit is purple.

I watch as the three of them each place a five dollar chip on the board. The numbers they pick look random. Brenda chose number three, Luis eighteen and Deanna zero. The dealer starts the ball, rolling around and around on the wheel. It lands in the number twenty-seven pocket. Nobody wins. I roll my eyes.

They repeat their bets, except now Brenda stupidly places a twenty-five dollar chip on number three. What a waste, she probably doesn't even see the difference in the chip amounts. I don't bother telling her and just keep drinking my wine. She's going to lose it anyway.

The ball freaking lands in the number three pocket. I don't believe it. She's squealing and jumping, her arms flailing around. Now she's being paid hundreds of dollars, which winds her up even more.

Good for her.

They all try one more bet, but no one wins, so we leave the table. Brenda is still glowing, and so is Luis for that matter. He must already be thinking they have joint finances.

We go to the main bar, which is huge compared to the others we've ordered from, where they have a band set up playing songs I've never heard before but have a nice tune.

Brenda and Luis are slow dancing to an upbeat song. Looks like they are pretty well suited to each other, both quirky in complimentary ways, moving to the beats of their hearts or something sappy like that.

Deanna tugs on my arm to get me to dance. I refuse. I haven't danced since Dave was alive. He would, on random nights, hug me from behind while I was doing the dishes, then spin me around to face him and we'd dance without music too. We'd seen it in a romance movie once and he made it a habit. We didn't get much closeness other than that. I miss it… I don't want to dance with anyone else and ruin the memory.

Then she waves over the young bartender girl that has cleavage popping out of her skimpy uniform, and tells her, "It's their engagement party." She points at Brenda and Luis dancing, "You guys do anything special for things like that?"

The bartender says, "Not really."

"Okay, beautiful. Thanks anyway." She winks at her.

"Actually, I could maybe get the band to do a shoutout and you can record it on your cell. Would that work?"

"Throw in a free drink and you've got a deal." She runs her finger over the bartender's hand.

The girl giggles, "What are their names?"

"Luis and Brenda."

"Okay, I'll see what I can do."

"Thanks, doll." She leans back in her chair like some macho man who's landed a date.

I say, "She's too young for you."

"Oh, I'm just havin' fun."

"Yeah right." I bet if she had the opportunity to go further, she would.

The bartender sneaks over to the band between songs and whispers in the singer's ear. Then she comes back, makes a quick phone call, then comes over to us, "Okay, they're going to do the shoutout then play a slow song. And we do have a special drink for couples, but I can't give it for free."

Deanna says, "That's okay, I got it." She pays for the drink, "But wait to bring it until after this song." She pulls out her cell phone and starts recording.

Then the singer speaks into the microphone, "All right everyone, this next song is for all those in love, so grab your partner and hold them close. One special couple this evening is celebrating their engagement. Congratulations, Luis and Brenna."

Of course they got her name wrong.

Wrapped in each other's arms, they turn to look at Deanna, mouthing the words, 'thank you'. Then they nestle into each other's necks.

Still recording, she moves closer to them and circles slowly around. Then the couple kisses like this is their first dance at their wedding or something. She got real close for that. I'm sorry, but, no one wants to see themselves kissing that close up, that's why people close their eyes.

As the song ends, Deanna makes her way back to her seat here at the bar, careful to keep the phone steady and aimed at Luis and Brenda, who giggle and walk toward us.

Then the bartender sets a tall colorful drink with two straws on the bar and says, "For the happy couple."

They start sipping on their drink at the same time. Deanna is still recording. The video will be a nice memory, now that i'm thinking about it. I wish I had one of Dave and I— Actually, I might have some videos, from our wedding at least. I'll have to go back up north and go through some things. So many memories up there. I'm also making memories here. It's too much in my brain. This life is so different, like I went to sleep one night and woke up a stranger to myself the next day and my old life is only a memory.

Now there's nothing left of the special couple's drink and Luis says, "Well, ladies. I think I've had too much. Why don't we make a night of it?"

Brenda says, "That sounds wonderful, my love!"

Deanna says, "I'm down!"

I shrug. I'm outnumbered and I don't feel like fighting with them. My family is dead no matter where I sleep.

The bartender says, "Go to the main desk and you can get a discount on your rooms at the motel next door."

Deanna says to the bartender, "You're the best. I'll come back and see you in a little bit then."

I roll my eyes.

Even discounted the rooms are too expensive, so in order to still have money to play with, Brenda and Luis are obviously sharing a room, and I'm going to share with Deanna. I know I could afford it, but it's not a purchase I can justify. I figure she'll be flirting with the bartender all night so I'll have the room to myself.

We walk to the next building over, which is almost attached to the casino. When I open the door to my and Deanna's room, there's only one king size bed. We specifically asked for two singles. Whatever, it doesn't matter, I want to go to sleep now the wine has made my head fuzzy.

I climb in bed and tell them to go on without me. They whine a little, but I insist, so they leave my room. I wish I had Annie's letter. I've gone to sleep reading her letter almost every night and it feels weird not to have it nearby at least, but I do have it memorized. I fall asleep during the second sentence.

∞ • ∞

I'm awakened. It feels like it's been hours. Wait, *am* I awake? No, I'm still dreaming because I can feel Dave behind me, his arms wrapped around me. I can feel his breath on my neck and his warmth along my back. Any minute now I'll hear my daughter come in to tell us she's made pancakes all on her own without burning down the house. I want to stay here forever in this moment.

Maybe this isn't a dream? Maybe losing them was

all a dream and I'm only now waking up from that nightmare. Without disturbing my husband, I pinch my arm. I'm definitely awake. I take a deep breath and let it out slow as I snuggle closer to him. I smile.

Thank God it was only a nightmare! I don't dare fall back asleep, so I look at the wall in front of me. It's different. Maybe I forgot what it looks like because of that horrible dream. Yeah, that must be it. I wonder if I should tell them that I dreamed they were dead. Nah, I don't want to drag it out, I'm just glad it's over. From here on out I'm going to make sure I show them how much I love and appreciate them.

There's a knock on the door. That must be my baby girl. She's always so respectful, my sweet baby girl. I try to speak just loud enough for her to hear me, "Come on in, Annie baby."

Dave rolls away from me and the door doesn't open. I sit up, slide out of bed. Okay, this is a hotel room, that's why the walls look different. We must be on vacation.

I open the door and see Brenda. I say, "Good morning, sis, where's Annie?" I look both ways down the hall, "She's not with you?"

"What?"

"Shh. Don't wake Dave, you know he needs his sleep. Where's Annie?"

Brenda has a funny look on her face and presses her hand against my forehead like she's feeling for a fever, then she comes into the room, walks over to the bed and flings the covers back.

I start to yell at her, but then I see Deanna sitting up where Dave was sleeping. My jaw drops. No, no, no, no, please, no. It was him, I swear it was! I mutter, "But

Dave was—he was right there…" I look back toward the door, "And I thought Annie was—" I cover my face with my hands. It's another dream. Wake up. Wake up! I close my eyes tight, then all at once uncover my face and open my eyes. They're staring at me. Brenda's coming in to hug me. I cover my face again.

She says, "Oh, May, you know they're gone. Their spirits are with you always, but you know they're not here anymore."

I push her off me, "Damn it, Brenda! I know. I know! I just need a minute."

"Okay, fine, I'll get Luis and we'll wait for you in the hall, but we need to get on the road soon."

"Just get out!"

She leaves the room. I look at Deanna and shout, "And you! What are you doing? Get out of my room!"

"This is our room, remember?"

"No! Get out!"

She moseys into the bathroom and shuts the door.

I sit on the bed. What is real? Is this reality? Please, God, I want to go back.

Ugh, that's right, I agreed to share a room. I remember everything and wrap my brain around my situation. I clench my fists. It's Deanna's fault that now I feel like I've lost Dave and Annie all over again! How dare she. It's Brenda's fault too, and Luis' for that matter. They're all ruining my life!

I storm out the door but the hallways is empty, and I don't wait for anyone either. I keep walking toward where I think Luis' van is parked. This motel is stupid. This casino is stupid. This parking garage is stupid. I can't find the van anywhere so I walk back to the casino and wait just inside the doors. I ought to call a cab. Yeah, I think I'll do that.

By the time I get outside, the cab is waiting. I get in, give the guy my address and we drive off.

CHAPTER THIRTY-ONE

Ready

When I get back to the house, the first thing I notice is the pavers are done, like I care anymore. Then I check on my birds. They're still guarding their nest. "Oh, Limpy, I'm having the worst day. I thought all of this was a nightmare and I finally woke up from it this morning only to find out that this nightmare is my life now. They're dead all over again!"

The birds don't even look up at me.

"Did you hear what I said? I could really use some support right now."

Nothing.

"Answer me!"

"Keow!" Limpy yells back at me.

"What is your problem? I just need someone to talk to!"

"Keow!" He screams and flies up onto the porch bannister right in front of my face.

I remember what happened last time when he lunged at me, so I take a step back and point my finger at him, "Stop that!"

"Keow! Keow!"

"Stop it, right now!"

He tries to bite my finger with his long curved beak which doesn't hurt my finger but does hurt my feelings.

"Fine! Screw you, you stupid bird!" I stomp down and over to the fence Deanna put up, and I start kicking it. My foot gets caught in the wire and I fall to the dirt. Wriggling around, I free my foot but my pants are stuck so I slide out of them. It's too hot for pants anyway. I take my top off too. Who cares if I'm in my underwear? Not me. I yell, "Screw you, sun!" Then I look down at the Limpkins, "Screw you, birds!"

I march toward the marsh but trip over a root of the oak tree. "Screw you, tree, and your stupid roots!" I stomp through the grass until my feet start sinking into the muck. An apple snail almost cuts my toes. "Screw you, snail!" I pick it up and throw it out into the water.

Standing at the water's edge, I turn my head to the sky and hold out my arms and scream as loud as I can for as long as I can in one breath. Then, after I catch my breath, I yell, "Why are you torturing me? What have I done to deserve this life?" I point at the sky, "Screw you too!"

Just then, a beetle crawls up my leg. I swat it off, but it's quickly replaced by a mosquito, then a fly. I smack my legs until I'm red, when I notice a bright orange butterfly. I straighten myself to watch it and end up stumbling backwards to free my feet from the mushy ground they've sunk into. A few steps back I'm on solid ground again and focused on the beautiful creature that's almost glowing in contrast to the darkening skies behind it. Thunder roars and in a flash of lightning the butterfly disappears.

"Now you're going to rain on me too? Sure! Why not? Like I haven't been through enough!"

The wind picks up, whipping my hair around my face and sending the tips of the tall marsh grasses into a frenzy. I plant my feet and ball my fists. Huge raindrops smack the earth around me, one by one, like a warning.

"Go ahead! I'm not afraid!"

With a crack of thunder, the drops amass to a waterfall from the heavens. My knees give out and I fall back into the mud, my body pelted with the water and pea-sized hail. I scramble to my feet and shield my head with my hands.

"Come on! Take me!"

My hair cuts across my eyes. It burns, but I steady myself and let my tears run away with the rain. A strike of lightning stretches across the sky, almost reaching out to me.

"Do it! I'm ready!"

Lightning strikes down in the center of the marsh with a force so great all of my hairs stand on end. My heart is racing as the energy surges through my body. I close my eyes tight and brace for the end.

∞ • ∞

I feel the sun on my face and open my eyes. The black clouds have been replaced by a blue sky, then the rain stops and everything looks as if there was never a storm at all. Everything but me.

Was that God answering me? Saying he could strike me down, but won't? "UGH!" I yell and stomp back toward the house. I walk up to the fence around Limpy's nest and glare at the birds who are shaking water droplets from their feathers like it was no big deal.

Ungrateful birds. I climb into the fenced area. Birdy flies up into the tree while Limpy is standing guard.

"Out of the way, so I can move your stupid nest away from *my* house!" I step closer and see behind him three baby Limpkins, all fuzzy and cute, and staring at me.

"So that's why you were being so rude. Fine, stay for now, but you better start showing some appreciation!"

Stepping back over the fence, my toe catches the top wire, "Damn it!" I plummet face first, my leg stuck in the air.

I'm so not in the mood for this. I lay here for a moment as the family of birds seem to judge me, but I don't care.

Then something slithers in the grass nearby. I spot it immediately, a freaking black snake, three feet long and staring at the babies. You've got to be kidding me. I jerk my leg to free myself, stand up and take a few steps back, then yell at Limpy, "You better get that snake!"

They're all focused on me while the snake slithers up to the fence and tastes the air with its tongue. Am I seriously the only one who sees it? Am I imagining it?

Oh, shit, Limpy spotted it. Get it! He's jumping and— "Where are you freaking going?" He's flown away, leaving his babies to fend for themselves. Now the babies are jumping around. The snake moves closer.

I look around for a stick or something I can smack it with, but there's no time. It's breached the fence and moving steadily closer. Screw this! I dash over and grab the serpent's tail just in time. I yank the snake out and in one fluid movement, fling it around and release it flying into the air, in the front yard.

Almost immediately I hear screaming. At first I think it's the baby birds, like maybe I missed and threw a stick or something, but it's coming from behind me. I turn around to see Brenda and Luis dodging the snake while Deanna is chasing after it like an exaggerated comedy act.

Laughter bursts out of me. That is the funniest thing I've ever seen! What are the chances?

Brenda yells at me, "Have you lost your mind!?"

I can't stop laughing, but I know I haven't, at least not all of it.

"What are you doing out here in your underwear, throwing snakes at people?"

"I was saving my ungrateful birds." Hearing the words come out of my mouth make me laugh even harder.

Deanna catches the snake and starts laughing with me. She gets it. Brenda's shaking her head, probably about to reprimand me for my behavior.

I say, "The eggs hatched. Want to see?"

"Absolutely!" says Deanna. She brings the snake with her. "Aw, such sweet little babies." Then she looks the snake in the eyes, "You don't mess with May's birds anymore, ya'hear?"

Taking a moment to gather my thoughts, I'm

struck by the absolute beauty of life despite the seemingly constant dangers. I couldn't prevent the death of my Annie or Dave, but I know I really am happy for the time I had with them. If God won't even strike me down, then maybe I'm supposed to start living again. Conquering my fear of snakes to save the baby birds seems like the perfect way to start. I think I get it now.

Then Brenda and Luis come over to see the babies. But instead of saying how cute they are, Brenda starts right in with, "We were worried sick about you, ya know?"

"I'm sorry, I needed some space. And look, you guys found me, so no harm done."

"But, you scared me to death!"

"Let it go. That's your problem, you can't move on. I'm fine, so why harp on me about every little thing?"

"Well, because you apparently need to learn how to be an adult again."

"Whatever." I get myself a beer and sit on the porch, still in my underwear.

Now Brenda and Luis are talking by the oak tree and Deanna's letting the snake loose in the brush by the far end of the driveway. Ordinarily, I would have yelled at her to drive it miles away, but I'm beginning to understand her view on nature. I'm not alone here on the marsh, so I need to learn to live with the creatures that come with it.

They all join me but I just keep looking out at the horizon, trying to hold on to this newfound feeling I have. Maybe this is what peace feels like?

Brenda goes inside, then brings out three more beers and a robe that she lays over me so I don't have to get up. We all smile at each other and sit in silence.

Then Deanna says, "Good job, by the way, handling that snake."

I raise my beer, then take a sip.

CHAPTER THIRTY-TWO

Preparations

A week has passed and I'm feeling better and better each day. I'm recognizing when the spirit of my Dave or Annie are with me, cherishing those moments, and thinking about what I want to do. Don't get me wrong, I still haven't done much. I've come to terms with the fact that I'm a millionaire now and I don't have to work if I don't want to.

I'll manage the money to live off the interest, then I'll never worry about running out, so long as I don't over-spend the interest amount for that year. Dave would be proud that I actually learned a thing or two from him. He knew all about what to do with money, if we ever got a lot, which we never did. But he liked to dream. Now, I can make his dreams come true for him and Annie's dreams come true for her. I've been given opportunities and I don't need to be so focussed on *why* I have the money. I need to focus on what I'm going to do with it.

But the more pressing issue, despite how annoying she still can be, is making sure Brenda has an enjoyable wedding. I'm pretty sure now that I am to blame for the wedge between us, because of how I was handling the loss of my family —which was not handling it at all.

Over the week, the exterior of my house has been painted by Luis, Deanna and a couple of her friends that owed her favors. Yep, my run-down Florida cracker house is now a beautiful soft green with white trim, which brings out the colors of the natural stone pavers. The arbor has been set up under the oak tree and overall my property went from sad to picturesque, not unlike my mood.

Now, Deanna's finishing planting the flowers and there's nothing left for me to do, so I'm going to visit Luis's in-laws because apparently they still refuse to come to the wedding. Ridiculous.

I arrive at a decent sized house and ring the doorbell. Three women open the door. I say, "Hi, I'm May Johnson, Brenda's sister. Can I come in?"

They let me in, but not with a smile.

"So, I hear you all don't agree with the wedding."

They mumble something in Spanish under their breaths.

Nice try. I know they understand me. I speak as clearly as I can, like a principal holding a staff meeting, "You are lucky that Luis fell in love with her. She is a sweet and loving person and will be a good mother to those kids. I don't know you all yet, but I've heard good things so I'm sure we will be happy to have you all as family too." I pause to let my words sink in. There's no change in their furrowed expressions though. "I hope you can find it in your hearts to attend the wedding and see Isabella, Sofia and Zoe as flower girls, and to at least support Luis. It's in two days, in case you forgot. I'll leave you with that and be on my way." I show myself the door, then turn around, "Hope to see you all there."

I sit in my car for a minute. That felt so good! Even if Brenda's not a natural mom, I'll be there to help her, with Dave and Annie's spirits to help me. Maybe that's another reason God won't take me yet: that I'm supposed to pass on my knowledge of married life and motherhood.

When I get back to my house, Deanna says, "Come here, I want to show you something," and leads me to the side of the arbor under the oak tree. Two crosses are planted in the ground like grave markers, one for Dave and one for Annie, both painted white.

I hold back tears as I hug her, "They're beautiful."

"I'm glad you like them, but I'm all sweaty so get off me." She winks.

"Yeah, you are. Go shower." I gaze at the crosses, almost testing to see if I can hold myself together. Then I remember, I'm already being held by a power greater than me, and I smile.

Then Limpy walks out from behind the tree with his three long-legged, fuzzy babies. They kind of remind me of cotton candy on a stick. They pass by me then circle back around toward the marsh. Guess they only wanted to say hello. It's amazing that they survive out here. Aw, Birdy just joined them and it looks like she's brought dinner.

Heading toward the house, I pause for a moment at the now abandoned nest to reminisce. It was only what, four or five months ago Limpy came into my life? In that short amount of time he found a mate and started a family. He changed my life too, now that I think about it, in little ways that maybe add up to something big. It's strange how things work out.

I sit in a rocking chair on the porch. It's hot outside but I guess I've acclimated to the weather and now I can't imagine dealing with snow again in my life, ever. I'm going to have to do something with my house and all my stuff up north though. Maybe I'll pay Brenda to pack it up.

Deanna joins me and hands me a beer, "Whatcha thinkin' about?"

"Stuff. I'm not sure what to do with my old life."

"Aw, you're not old yet, pussycat."

"Thanks, but not what I meant." I slap her arm. "My house up north."

She laughs. "You only have so many options to choose from: Keep it and let it rot away over time, sell it, though it's not like you need the money, or give it away and let it help someone, so long as you don't owe too much on it still."

Hm. I think the house is almost paid off actually. That does simplify things… I'll have to brew on it. "Hey, speaking of old, whatever happened with you and that bartender you're too old for?"

"Ha. Ha. Very funny."

"Well?"

"You jealous?"

"Now you're the funny one!"

"It was only some flirting, that's all. It's not every day a pretty girl actually puts up with me."

I throw my hands out and sarcastically say, "What about me?"

"Besides you." She winks. "You ever think about dating again?"

"Dee, I'm not a lesbian."

"Yeah, I know, you've reminded me enough. I mean dating in general."

I sigh, "Nah, I'm not ready. I still feel married to my Dave and maybe I always will. He was the only person I've ever been with, so I wouldn't even know where to begin with someone new at my age."

"No shit. Really? You haven't been with anyone else?"

I shake my head.

"Damn."

"He was the love of my life."

"You're lucky. Most people never get the chance."

"Yeah, well, I wouldn't wish losing the love of your life on anyone. We were supposed to grow old together. Now what the hell am I going to do? Set myself a reminder to check myself into an assisted living facility before I lose my mind?"

"That's how it is for a lot of people. I mean, come on, pussycat, you don't think you're the only one in the world in your situation do you?"

"It feels like it."

Deanna cups my face in her hands, touches her nose to mine and whispers like some crazy alien conspirator, "You're not alone." Then her face changes. "That reminds me, I know a gal who's a little," she draws a circle with her finger in the air next to her head. "But, she's a photographer and wants to get into doing weddings. She would be grateful for some work for her portfolio. What do you think?"

"You know everyone don't you?"

"Well, when you extract gators and whatnot from people's properties, they tend to want to keep in touch. So what do you say?"

"Honestly? I hadn't even thought about it. It's kind of late notice."

"Oh, she'd do it."

"All right then, it's better than nothing."

She turns the page of an invisible book in her hands, "Next order of business: What are you going to wear?"

"Ugh, I hadn't thought about that either... My track suit?"

"No."

Hm, I'll have to find something in town tomorrow.

"I see you thinking about it, but let me stop you." She's grinning. "Brenda and I already picked out your dress."

"What the hell! It better not be tight, or frilly, or too short, or too—"

"Relax. You'll like it. It's simple and comfortable."

Great. I might end up wearing my track suit after all. I can't believe the wedding is in two days already. Luis' family better show up, or I'll be paying them another visit. Better yet, I'll keep going over there until I wear them down. It'll be my little project, along with shopping for the girls—"Shit! Flower girl dresses!"

"Oh, man. Shit is right, I completely forgot!" She pulls out her phone and starts typing.

A moment later her phone dings, "Okay, we're cool. Brenda said she took the girls shopping with her winnings from the casino."

"Seriously? I agreed to pay and she goes behind my back and buys their dresses? Ask her how much it was."

She types on her phone, then when it dings she reads aloud, "If you're asking for May, I'm not telling."

"Well, I'll figure out a way to get her back."

"Yeah, okay, pussycat. You do that. She'll be here soon to stay the night, and I'm sleeping on the couch, so good luck getting past me. That's right, she told me about the taser incident."

"Not one of my finer moments, but I still laugh about it when I think back. You know, since she didn't get seriously hurt or anything." I sigh, "We've come a long way."

"Don't ever taser me." She laughs.

"No, I think those days are over."

CHAPTER THIRTY-THREE

Family

Today is the big day and I actually truly feel happy for Brenda. Part of me expected her to be neurotic and overall unpleasant about having everything perfect today, but she's been so patient, especially with the kids, even letting them help style her hair while she puts her makeup on.

Since we are in my bedroom, Deanna is in her bedroom helping Luis get dressed. His in-laws didn't bother showing up, which is a shame, but what more could we do? I thought at least his sister-in law would attend, since she was always supportive. Oh well, there's folding chairs outside, waiting to be set up, just in case.

The dining room is ready to display cupcakes I

had ordered, but of course they're not here yet. I'm not going to stress about it though, they're only cupcakes, and there's still time. Whenever I mention yet another thing that's not perfect for her day, Brenda tells me, "All that matters is love." She's right.

I peek in on Luis and Deanna, "How's it going in here?" They're both dressed in dark blue suits with yellow ties.

Deanna dabs sweat off the grooms forehead. "Will you please tell this man that your sister is still here."

"She's here and excited as ever."

He nods and takes a deep breath.

I take a deep breath too. "So, I wanted to ask you, before everything gets going, if um...would you mind introducing me to a grief counseling group sometime? Whenever you get the chance."

Luis hugs me, "Of course! I'm so happy for you, that's a very big step in the right direction."

"And don't let me back out of it, okay?"

"You have my word."

Deanna hugs me too, "You know I'll go with you if you want."

"I'd like that."

She checks the time on her watch, "Oh, the photographer should be here by now."

There's a knock on the front door. That must be her. I open the door to find it's the cupcakes and the photographer too. She's out there bobbing around getting pictures of the arbor and flowers.

I help get the cupcakes set up, though really all I did was point my finger a couple of times. Then, as the delivery people are leaving, the photographer comes in. I direct her to Deanna's bedroom then I dash into mine.

"The photographer is here. We need to get the girls dressed."

Brenda eyes me up and down, "You need to shower."

Shit. I hurry into the bathroom.

She hollers, "Shave, please!"

"Ugh, fine!"

Twenty minutes later I'm getting out of the shower. Shaving my legs was like trying to cut grass with a shovel, but I got most of it. At the very least, it's obvious I made an effort.

The dress I'm supposed to wear looks decent enough, though not exactly what I would have picked out. It's a soft yellow sundress that falls just below my knees, with a dark blue ribbon wrapped around the waist. Blue and yellow like Luis and Deanna's suits and ties. I think I like it. It fits pretty good too, not tight but not like a trash bag either. A quick blow-dry on my hair and I'm ready.

I throw some of Brenda's makeup on my face as she's carefully sliding her wedding dress on. My heart skips when she turns around. It's happening, my little sister is getting married.

The photographer comes in and starts photographing Brenda as she pretends to apply her makeup that's already done, with the girls huddled around. Their dresses are so cute, made of alternating blue and yellow fabric that looks like netting, woven together and cinched with a ribbon around the waist, like my dress, only theirs then poof out above and below the ribbon, down to their knees like a tutu. They are like beautiful little ballerinas.

Now I'm supposed to pretend I'm zipping up

Brenda's dress, but it's weird to have my picture taken. My smile feels awkward. I feel like I should suck in my stomach, but when I do my neck muscles tense up and there's no way that'll be a good picture.

Brenda whispers, "Just breathe."

I'm suddenly calm. I remember when I said that to her at my wedding. Today isn't about me and it doesn't matter that I'm not model material. These are memories. New, beautiful memories, despite what I look like in them.

∞ • ∞

Time to start the ceremony before we lose daylight. The photographer goes out front to get set up and make sure her assistant is ready to record everything on video. I summon Luis and Deanna and we all go out front together.

Our jaws drop when we open the door. They came! They all came! Luis runs down the steps and starts hugging everyone while Deanna and I help set up the chairs. They all seem to be in good spirits too, not like they're here out of obligation.

Luis' sister-in-law approaches me and explains how she helped win them over, but it was my speech to them that opened the door to acceptance. Some of them, whose names I don't even know, actually hugged me too.

Deanna starts playing some instrumental music from her phone that's connected to speakers somewhere, though I couldn't say where. Luis takes his position in front of Deanna under the arbor, everyone is seated, and I'm off to send out the flower girls.

Should I tell Brenda about the family? Well, I

think she's going to cry either way. I'll let her be surprised. I make her stay in the bedroom while I send Isabella out first. Then Sofia and last but not least, little Zoe.

A moment later I try to send Brenda, but she grabs my arm and whispers, "Please, will you walk me?" She's crying already.

I wipe her tears, "I'd be honored."

"How is Luis?"

"Nervous."

"Oh no, like he's not sure he wants to go through with it?"

"No, he's worried maybe you won't."

She giggles and takes a few deep breaths as I tidy her bouquet in her trembling hands.

I ask, "Are you ready?"

She nods and I open the door. Deanna changes the music to a beautiful, though unconventional version of the traditional 'Here Comes the Bride' song. Everyone turns to look at us and Brenda shrinks like she's going to collapse, but I catch her and help keep her upright.

"May, they're all here. Do you see them too?"

"Yes, this is real."

She takes a deep breath and we walk arm in arm down the aisle, past all the smiling faces of family. Then I kiss her on the cheek as I leave her by Luis' side and take my seat with the flower girls. I gaze at Dave and Annie's crosses and imagine my husband and daughter sitting next to me.

Deanna speaks, "Ladies and gentlemen, family and friends, we are gathered here today to witness and celebrate the joining of Luis Garcia and Brenda Hall in marriage. And as we create this marriage, we also create a new bond and new sense of family, one that will undoubtedly include all who are present today."

She pauses for a moment, then continues, "Luis and Brenda, may you succeed in all important ways with each other, and not fail in the little graces. May you have happiness, and may you find it in making each other happy. May you always have hope in your hearts and find the light in darkness. May you have love, and find it in loving one another. May you always bear in mind that when you love someone, you do not love them all the time, in exactly the same way, from moment to moment. And may you always have May. See what I did there?"

Me, Brenda and Luis giggle. The girls laugh too, though I don't think they understand why. Then I notice Limpy, Birdy and their babies sitting in the big oak tree, above the arbor, as if they have the best seats in the house to watch the ceremony.

Deanna continues, "There is an ebb and flow in life, love and relationships. The highs and lows are a package deal. Grow together, support one another, and remember this day and the vows you made to each other." She holds out her hand to Luis to signal the time for him to read his vows.

He clears his throat, pulls out a piece of paper from his pocket and reads, "Brenda, the moment I saw you I knew my life would never be the same. After my wife passed, God rest her soul, I didn't know if or how I could ever love again, but you showed me. You showed me with your loving spirit, your patience and kindness to my daughters, and your acceptance of me as I am. I vow to love you always, no matter what."

I hand Brenda the vows she wrote, and she reads, "Luis, I thought I would never have a family of my own.

Then you walked in that front door." She points to the house. "I knew we would have something special and when I learned of your daughters, I felt like I won the lottery. I promise to always respect their mother in Heaven, while trying my best to love and care for them as she would. I vow to love you always, no matter what." She turns to the audience, "We didn't plan that last line, by the way." She laughs.

Luis says, "We really didn't, but that just shows our connection." He leans in to kiss her.

Deanna sticks her hand between them, "Hey, hey, not 'til I say so."

Everyone laughs.

Then Deanna gives Luis and Brenda the rings to exchange. "Repeat after me: I give you this ring."

The bride and groom speak in unison, "I give you this ring."

"As a visible and constant symbol."

"As a visible and constant symbol."

"Of my promise to be with you, for as long as I live."

"Of my promise to be with you, for as long as I live."

"Now, by the power vested in me by the state of Florida, I pronounce you husband and wife. Now you can kiss your bride, Luis."

The newlyweds embrace each other, lips locked together and tears streaming down their cheeks. The audience, myself included, all stand and applaud. Deanna starts up the music to play a joyful instrumental song.

The bride and groom face us with hands joined in the air and smiles stretching across their faces. A tear streams down my cheek. I didn't think I would cry, but here I am, and through my teary vision, I swear I can see my Dave and Annie standing off to the side, clapping joyously.

∞ ● ∞

The sun is setting and casting a gorgeous warm glow, but before we do pictures the bride and groom want to feed each other a cupcake inside. So we all quickly gather in the living room. Brenda and Luis are so gentle I don't think they dropped a crumb.

Deanna pops open a bottle of champagne and I help her make sure everyone has a glass. Then I stand next to the bride and groom, and clink a spoon on my glass. The room quiets and now all eyes are on me.

"For anyone who doesn't know me, I'm May, Brenda's sister. For the ones that do know me, this is not something I would normally do after... I've been dealing with the loss of my own family, and—" I clear my throat. Come on, hold it together. "Well, anyway, I just want to say I truly am happy these two found love. My sister and I are all that's left of our family, but we welcome you all and I hope you welcome us too. Thank you and congratulations to the bride and groom."

"Hear, hear!" Deanna cheers.

"Oh, wait! One more thing, my wedding gift is... my house up north. Do with it what you want and all I ask is that you ship my stuff down to me."

Brenda looks faint, then her champagne glass slips from her hand. Without thinking, I reach out and catch it as Luis holds her up.

She says, "Wow, May...I mean, I'll gladly do the work for you, but it's too much."

"It's a gift. You can't refuse." I wink. "I just hope you consider selling it and staying in Florida."

She wraps her arms around me and whispers, "I love you."

I whisper back, "I love you too."

Luis taps on his glass, "I'd like to make a toast. To May. Without you, Brenda and I might never have met, and we wouldn't all be here today. You're a blessing to us all and I am forever thankful." He raises his glass.

Deanna shouts, "To May, to Brenda and Luis, to family and friends, to life, and to love! Hear, hear!"

We all raise our glasses and drink, then gather outside for a group picture in front of the sunset over the marsh. This one is definitely going on my night table.

About the Author

E.J.Stillings believes anything is possible with a little courage, kindness and persistence. After graduating high school, she pursued several creative endeavors until finally, a bird gave her clarity. She narrowed her focus and now that same bird is featured in her debut novel, *The Crying Bird*.

Her stories may be works of fiction, but her characters experience the same events that encompass the human condition, a subject she loves to analyze. She lives with her life partner and rescue cats in the city where she was born and raised, Orlando Florida.

Connect with E.J.Stillings
Website: ejstillings.com
Social Media: facebook.com/ejstillings

If you enjoyed this book, please consider writing a review.
Thank you!

Made in the USA
Columbia, SC
28 March 2022